FLASHES OF INSIGHT

LYNDA ALLEN

LIVING HEARTFULLY PRESS

For permission requests, contact Living Heartfully Press at: PO Box 7285, Fredericksburg, VA 22404 or livingheartfullypress@lyndaallenwrites.com

Library of Congress Control Number: 2024900627

ISBN (paperback): 978-1-7322557-4-6

ISBN (eBook): 978-1-7322557-5-3

This is a work of fiction. All of the characters, locations, events, or organizations portrayed are either a product of the author's imagination or are used fictitiously.

Book Cover by Laura Boyle

First edition: 2024

To

Bill, who loves and accepts G.G. with humor and heart.

All the G.G.s who feel unseen and unheard.

Dad, who always believed in my creative endeavors.

CHAPTER ONE

It used to irritate me when people thought they knew something about me based on which New Jersey Turnpike exit was nearest to where I grew up. Then I went through a phase of telling people which exit to hell they could use when they trotted out that tired joke. Now I've lived in Virginia for more than twenty-five years, and most people don't even know I'm from Jersey. At least not until they've had the pleasure of hearing my array of colorful expletives or until they've met G.G.

G.G. is short for Grumpy Gal. She arrived with the onset of perimenopause, along with a handful of other heartwarming side effects like hot flashes, insomnia, and weight fluctuations— that's a nice way of saying weight gain. I didn't have a nickname or euphemism for the other side effect of perimenopause, the life-changing one. The one I'd never heard of anyone else experiencing. I mean, I'd never heard it would make my elbows sweat either, but psychic visions in the middle of hot flashes? They were definitely not listed as a side effect in any of the articles I'd read.

It was one of those visions, which arose during yoga last week, that made me wonder if I was losing my grip on reality.

I went to my first yoga class in my early fifties. Not because it was trendy, but because I sit on one of my best assets all day while working. So, I needed to do some stretching to balance out all the chair-time. Thanks to another attractive perimenopause side effect, untimely flatulence, it was nearly my first and last class.

My friend Sophie Grace and I chose Posers in downtown Fredericksburg, Virginia because the name made us laugh, and pretty much anything that makes us laugh gets our attention. We were doing a pose called Pavanamuktasana in Sanskrit. It would have gone a long way toward easing my mind if our instructor Angie had called it by its name in English, "wind-relieving pose." It's an apt description. You lie on your back and pull one knee up to your chest (as close as you can at least) and, you guessed it, the "wind" in your digestive tract is released. If you're lucky—or dainty, I suppose—it's released quietly. Unfortunately, during our first session, my wind was anything but quiet or dainty upon its release. Sophie and I were laughing so hard we had to leave. It's a wonder we ever got up the nerve to go back, but luckily Angie has a sense of humor too. I still smile to myself whenever we get to that pose.

What I would have given for a little levity in our class last week instead of the vision. If I'd had a better idea of what was happening to me, that what I was having were truly prescient insights, the following week might have turned out differently, less life-threateningly.

CHAPTER TWO

H e resented names. Names could hold power, or they could hold shame. It didn't matter if it was your shame or your father's or an ancestor's from long ago. Their shame could still cling to you, like the damp silks from corn clung to his fingers as a child when he sat on the porch shucking on a summer evening. No matter how much you shook your hand, those silks wouldn't come off on their own. They had to be removed intentionally.

Some names had weight to them. Names like Washington, Madison, and Monroe. Good Virginia gentlemen from good Virginia families. Washington and Monroe had a lot of visibility in this town, Washington in particular. He'd heard about him all his life growing up in Fredericksburg. Yet the high school he'd attended had been named not for Washington, but for James Monroe, and it was Monroe who captivated his attention now.

James Monroe, fifth President of the United States. Many overlooked him, yet he was present at or party to so many pivotal events in the early Republic and the world. A wounded warrior in the American Revolution. Instrumental in securing the

Louisiana Purchase. In attendance at Napoleon's coronation. Secretary of State and Secretary of War simultaneously during the War of 1812, two-term President of the United States, the Monroe Doctrine, the Missouri Compromise. The list of his accomplishments was long, and yet history glossed over him, undervalued him. He died with relatively little money for his stature. He'd run up debts while serving in his official capacities, which were never fully repaid.

Oh, yes, he'd learned a lot more about Monroe since he made his discovery. *Overlooked and undervalued.* He might not be able to relate to Monroe's ability to speak several languages, or his stature as landed gentry, but he could relate to that.

He gently ran a finger over the nearly 200-year-old pieces of delicate, folded parchment in his hands, knowing there was a chance for Monroe to reach out through time and help him reverse his family's fortunes. In the process, he might be able to return the favor and help elevate Monroe's legacy. At least indirectly. He did have some hesitation, considering the kind of people he would likely have to deal with. They might not be interested in sharing his discovery with the world, especially given the means he might have to go to in order to obtain it. He knew a class of collectors existed who were more interested in their private collections and the notoriety it gave them in particular circles than they were interested in illuminating the historical record.

He'd been frustrated at first by his mother's request to go through some old boxes in the attic two months ago, but he did love history, even if he hated his own. So eventually, he found himself enjoying the process of going through the letters, books, photos, documents, memorabilia, and press clippings. A lot of it he'd seen or at least heard about before, but she had acquired two boxes of things when his father's sister, Mabel, died. Those items were all new to him. The letter in his hand was tucked between the pages of an old family Bible at the bottom of one of the boxes. He had been able to tell it was old just by looking at it.

When he read it through yet again, he imagined Margaret, his grandmother with too many greats before her name to count, sitting up in bed, gravely ill and writing out the words her daughter had obviously never received.

My darling Mae,

How I hope this message won't be necessary and that I will live to see my grandchildren full-grown. Yet, I cannot ignore the concern on Doctor Stewart's face, or the exhaustion I feel. If my time is indeed near to rejoin your father, my dear daughter, I must ensure a secret of the utmost importance makes it into your safekeeping. It is a secret entrusted to me by my dear friend Eliza.

It is hard for me to believe it was only three weeks ago I sat in perfect health beside the window in the parlor, gazing out onto Charles Street, waiting to catch sight of the wagon bringing Eliza's cherished treasure to me.

I could not help but remember a carriage drawn by two horses arriving on another fall day forty-four years previously. It was the day when I first caught sight of young Eliza, her belly swollen with child, alighting from the carriage in front of Mr. Jones's house.

I had been elated by the news that Mr. Jones's nephew, James Monroe, and his new wife, Elizabeth, would be moving to Fredericksburg and had been eagerly anticipating their arrival for weeks. I knew it would be a good place for a young lawyer to make a start and his uncle's stature in the community and in the state would help. The name of Joseph Jones would definitely open doors for him.

As you know, dear Mae, we became fast friends not long after their arrival. I admit I enjoyed introducing Eliza to the right people in town and taking her to the best shops for cloth and household supplies. We dined together, shared the challenges of motherhood, laughter, and even shared secrets.

It is one of those secrets I have to share with you now. It had become clear to Eliza during the last year that her health was failing. She had been dealing with health issues for years. Cruel people had whispered about her being aloof once James became president, but she was simply a private person and was appalled at the idea she might be seized during a state dinner or formal function. She didn't want her health issues to become the subject of gossip and cast a shadow over her dear James's presidency.

Her dear James. He is at the heart of the secret I share with you now. As a young bride, Eliza had hidden away the correspondence she received from James while they had been courting. After we became friends, she showed me how she had hidden them inside the hollow body of her harp. Years later, when James was serving his first term as president, I visited her at Oak Hill, their home in the countryside. During my visit, she took me aside to ask me a favor.

She couldn't have been prouder of James and his long career in politics. With his role in the founding of our nation, she understood there would be interest in his life and correspondence after he was gone, as there was after dear President Washington's passing. You'll recall much ado was made when Martha Washington burned all the correspondence between her and her husband following his death. James and Eliza were both extremely private people, so she knew he would want to do the same, but she also knew he was unaware of the letters she had hidden away. She had added more letters he'd sent her to the collection over the years, in addition to drafts of letters she had written to him. They had such a close and loving relationship and he relied on her perspective and insights into matters great and small, so his letters were a treasure to her.

That day at Oak Hill, she showed me the clever way she had contrived to hide the letters in plain sight inside her music book rather than inside her old harp. James knew how she loved to play the pianoforte and so, had taken all her favorite music and had it bound in one large book. A gift given to her with such love from James was the perfect place for Eliza to hide the letters.

She asked me to become the caretaker of the letters after her death. She pleaded with me to help her keep them secret until long after she and James were gone. She feared if she left them to one of her daughters, they would show them to James, and he would destroy them. She knew she couldn't guarantee how history would remember her husband, but she wanted to do what she could to show the world the loving, gentle, introspective man he was.

I couldn't refuse her and promised to follow her plan. She wrote to me not long before she died to remind me of my promise. She left the music book to me in her will and their trusted man, Tom, delivered it to me just a few weeks ago while on a trip to pick up supplies in Fredericksburg.

Oh, Mae, how my hand does tremble! I pray you can make out these words and that I can manage a few more. After Tom left, I sat in the sunlight at the parlor window and checked to be certain the letters were still there and took one precaution of my own to help ensure no one would find them until the right time. And now I fear there will be no right time, that the letters will be lost to history. I trust if my time has come, this letter will indeed make it into your hands so Eliza's secret can be revealed at the right time. I beg you to honor my dying request as well as Eliza's, while at the same time I pray I will live to honor it myself.

With Love Always,

Mother

He'd been disappointed to find the music book wasn't with his aunt's things, but if the story in the letter was true, his and Monroe's fortunes might be looking up. All he had to do was find the music book.

CHAPTER THREE

I don't know if it was part of the premonition or just a coincidence, but we were lying on our mats in corpse pose (what genius thought up that name?) when the vision began.

One of the great things about yoga classes, besides the laughter, is the deep relaxation at the end of each class. It's usually at least fifteen minutes, but on really good days, it's twenty. We go through the process of tensing and relaxing all the muscles in our body one after the other. Then Angie guides us through a soothing meditation for the remainder of the time while we concentrate on our breath. Normally it's heavenly. Normally.

I was lying there focusing on my breath when I felt the familiar hellfire start to blaze in the center of my upper back. I was used to the hot flashes, which I'd been having for five years or so.

It was only in the past few months I'd noticed a strange shift in the process. After the heat would kick in and the sweat would start beading on my elbows and in other places, which I'm too damn ladylike to mention (though rearrange the letters in elbow and you'll get the idea), something else would happen.

I'd started to have a kind of unsettled feeling at the center of my chest, and the hairs on the nape of my neck would stand up. Then an image of a person or an object would appear in my mind. Once, I envisioned someone I hadn't seen in years, who called me the next day. In a vision last month, I saw Sophie putting her phone in the pocket of a green, zip-up hoodie jacket as she went outside for the newspaper. She told me later the same day she couldn't find her phone. I asked if she'd checked her green hoodie with the frog on the front, and that's exactly where she ended up finding it. The thing was, she had just bought the jacket the previous day. I hadn't seen it yet. When she realized that, her reaction to my detailed description was a mixture of awe and what felt like wariness. It made me shiver.

Lying on my mat last week was the first time what I saw in a vision scared me, in no small part because it was also the first time it was about me. I was on Falmouth Bridge, one of the two bridges in Fredericksburg that cross the Rappahannock River. The water in the river was high, rushing by below me. I was leaning over the railing of the bridge. Leaning dangerously far. Then I was falling. Falling. Falling toward the dark water. My whole body jerked in an effort to stop my fall and I found I was on my mat in the present, drenched in sweat which no longer had anything to do with the hot flash. It frightened me so much, all I wanted to do was run home to see my neighbor, Lucia, my go-to person for anything unexplainable or mystical.

Sophie wanted to chat after class as usual, but I put an abrupt end to the conversation. I couldn't stop thinking about the rushing water. Sophie waved goodbye with an eye roll, saying, "Ok, G.G. I'll see you Friday."

My girlfriends are well-acquainted with Grumpy Gal.

I let G.G. take the blame for the abruptness, not wanting to stop to explain. All I wanted to do was talk to Lucia.

She and I had started out as acquaintances of proximity. Our townhouses are in a series of connected buildings next to the library downtown. They form their own small community. We all know one another by sight and by name, and beginning last spring, several of us had taken to hanging out in the shared courtyard on warm evenings. My friendship with Lucia has deepened since then because we truly enjoy each other's company. Having women in my life whose company I enjoy is essential.

I didn't even bother to go home to drop off my mat. Instead, I went directly to Lucia's door and rang the doorbell, not at all sure what I was going to say. Luckily, I didn't have to say a word. She opened the door, took one look at me, and reached out for my shoulder.

"Oh, my dear. Please come in and sit down. Are you all right?"

I felt slightly embarrassed to be found standing on her doorstep, apparently resembling a frightened child, but I didn't know what else to do, so I let her usher me inside.

We entered on the main level, passed the kitchen and dining area, and went to the living room. The large room had three tall windows, which instead of having a view of the street like mine did, overlooked the library.

I let her lead me to the couch upholstered in a lovely deep burgundy, which matched an accent wall in the room.

She said, "Wait here," and proceeded to the kitchen.

I flopped onto the couch and dropped my mat at my feet.

Lucia came back moments later with a glass of water. I accepted it, grateful for the coolness of the water and for the opportunity to gather myself drinking it allowed. As I sipped from it, I could hear the electric kettle heating up in the kitchen. Lucia sat with me as I collected my thoughts, her hand on my shoulder. Simply being in her presence was calming. It was one of the things I loved about her.

"Better?" she asked as I set the glass down on the coffee table.

"Yes, thank you."

There was a click from the kitchen. She patted my shoulder and left the room. I soon heard the clink of cups. It was the now-familiar sound of her making tea. She returned with a tray holding a full tea setting, including a teapot with steam rising from the spout. We sat in companionable silence for a few minutes, watching the steam rise.

Eventually Lucia scooted forward on the couch and poured tea into delicate white cups trimmed with the same deep burgundy color as the couch and wall. After pouring, she hesitated and said, "Hold on a second. I have just the thing."

She rose and walked to a wooden cabinet sitting on top of a bookshelf positioned between two of the windows. She opened the cabinet and removed an object from it. As she returned to the couch, I saw she was holding a bottle of Redbreast Irish Whiskey.

I was surprised, but grinned.

"This just became the best damn tea party I've ever been to," I said.

Lucia grinned too, and sitting beside me, poured a healthy shot of whiskey into our cups. We raised them in a toast.

I paused to breathe in the earthy scent of the red rooibos tea—she knew it was my favorite—blending with the scent of the whiskey. I took a sip. The heat that warmed me from the inside out reminded me of why I was there.

She must have seen the shift in my expression because her smile faded as she watched me over the top of her cup.

"What is it?" she asked. When I hesitated, she set down her cup with authority, fixing me with a gaze I couldn't shy away from. "Tell me the truth, Liv. What's going on?"

I had another quick sip of my fortifying tea and before I knew what I was doing, the words flooded out of me. I shared all the odd things I'd started experiencing in the midst of hot flashes.

"At first, it only happened in my dreams. I'd be awakened by what felt like a hot flash, but it was different. It wasn't accompanied by anxiety, which was the usual signal one was coming on. Instead, I would wake with an odd feeling."

"Odd how?" she asked.

"I can't really name it. It's sort of a combination of things. A kind of peaceful knowing, but frequently accompanied by a sense of foreboding. Peaceful foreboding? Is that a thing?" I felt like an idiot and glanced at her for reassurance.

She nodded for me to continue.

"Then the sensations started coming while I was awake, and they were usually accompanied by a vivid image in my mind, and still the sweating, of course. It began with what seemed like random things, thinking of someone I hadn't seen in a while, or I could see myself talking to someone on the sidewalk. If it had been lottery numbers, it might have been useful. Instead, it was a little creepy. The person I hadn't seen in a while called the next day to tell me a mutual friend from our childhood had passed away. Then, in the middle of that conversation on the sidewalk, which I did actually have later in the week, I remembered seeing it already and broke off the conversation."

I hadn't yet dared to tell anyone about the visions, especially given Sophie's reaction when she found her phone, and I realized I felt such relief to finally talk about them. Finally, I described the vision that had driven me to her door. The bridge. Stretching my arms out toward something and falling. The fear.

She let my words and my fears flow until they both ran out. I'd been saying so much so quickly, I was out of breath by the end, yet I felt calmer too. The fear gripping me had dissipated somewhat by sharing it.

I took another deep draw on my teacup and rested it on my leg, not quite fearless enough to make eye contact with her yet.

So, Lucia met me where I was. She reached out and put her hand on my arm. I studied her manicured nails, the wrinkles and thinning skin on her hands and forearm, the delicate gold ring in the shape of an infinity symbol, which wove itself from her middle finger to the ring finger on her right hand. I'd never seen anything like it.

She must have followed my gaze. "I had it made by a friend years ago. It was an image that came to me in a dream," she said.

I finally focused on her, only now noticing my eyes were damp with tears. When she began to speak, her tone was gentle and tinged with sadness. "So many women are made to think the natural processes occurring in their bodies and minds from menstruation through menopause are punishments, curses even. They've been sequestered in red tents, whispered about, and made to feel ashamed and dirty somehow." She patted my hand and smiled. "The tragedy is the exact opposite is true. These things are gifts." She held up her hand as I started to protest. "They are gifts of understanding, of empathy, of strength. They are part of the marvel of woman's ability to bring forth human life, but also of her ability to endure, to persevere, and to thrive despite challenge and even pain."

Her voice took on a melodious quality. "They are the embodiment of the power of nature. The tumultuous, molten fires of Earth's youth that first brought forth life onto this planet. The strength to move tectonic plates. A woman's curves mimic Earth's mountains, valleys, and deep ocean troughs, reflecting the heights of her spirit and the depths of her soul. The shaking of her foundations leading to menopause are a sign of growth and transformation just as earthquakes and volcanic eruptions are. The ever-changing landscape of woman is an echo of the ever-changing landscape of the Earth, which has wrought such beauty and natural wonders."

My jaw was hanging open. I'd never heard anything I thought was so beautiful and so ridiculous at the same time. I had nothing equally beautiful to say in response, so I simply raised my cup in salute.

"I hope I can see it that way someday. Right now, I could do with less molten lava and fewer eruptions of all kinds."

Her giggle started out quiet, but soon we were roaring with laughter and drinking a variety of toasts to womanhood and trying to figure out what parts of Earth represented men. I proposed it was the tar pits or those gaseous vents at the bottom of the ocean, but she was kinder than me and suggested the warmth and beauty of the shifting desert sands.

I leaned in confidentially. "We both know they would say it's the mighty sequoias, when weeping willows would be more accurate."

Once we caught our breath, she raised her cup solemnly and maintained a somewhat straight face. "To the mighty sequoias. Long may their wood stand proud and tall!" We clinked our cups together and fell back on the couch, laughing and sighing.

After a pause, she sat up and refilled our teacups with tea and whiskey. She lounged against the arm of the couch.

"You know what you're having?" She didn't wait for a response but plunged on. "You're having flashes of insight."

I let that sink in. It was odd because I didn't feel a need to dispute the statement. It felt like a fact. "OK, but what do they mean? If they're premonitions of things to come, what the hell did the one today mean?"

She was thoughtful momentarily, before saying, "It's not for me to say. From what I've learned about premonitions or psychic abilities over the years, they can provide detailed information about an event that might transpire, or they can be messages that need to be deciphered. They can offer guidance or a warning."

My heartbeat quickened at the word "warning."

"It varies greatly from person to person. I'm afraid you'll need to learn as you go, listening carefully to your inner teacher, your inner guide."

Between Lucia and Angie, I'd been told about this mysterious inner teacher many times, but try though I had, the method for listening to it still felt elusive. I was pretty confident my inner teacher had suspended me.

I put down my teacup. "But why me? Why now?" I tried to keep the whine I was feeling out of my voice.

"I think it's safe to assume because of the link to your hot flashes, that it's caused by the variations in your hormones brought on by perimenopause. All sorts of things change when we move through the cycles of hormonal shifts in our lives. It starts with puberty. Then many women experience dramatic transformations with pregnancy, perimenopause, and menopause, like fluctuations in their hair texture, body odor, complexion, moodiness—"

I interrupted. "I'm vaguely familiar with that one."

She smiled, having met G.G. during the course of our friendship.

I'd learned a lot about Lucia, since we'd become friends. She'd never been married, but she'd had several passionate love affairs, one of which was ongoing and one of which led to a beautiful daughter and now grandchildren she adored. There was a love of her life, but they had met at the wrong time. He'd been married when they met in her forties and although they considered an affair, she didn't want to be the cause of regret for him in breaking his vows. Their connection was deep, and they still occasionally reached out to each other. But he had grandchildren of his own and was deeply rooted in his family circle, which she had no desire to intrude upon. Though it was different from the loss of my husband, Nate, the loss of the love of her life was one of the things that bonded us together.

"I've never heard of psychic abilities being awakened by a hormonal change later in life, but that doesn't mean others haven't had similar experiences. It's possible, since you've already been experiencing hot flashes for some time and yet the visions are relatively new, that it's the final shift from perimenopause into menopause that's prompted them. You're officially becoming a crone," she said, grinning.

"Oh, God. As if G.G. wasn't bad enough, now I'm an old crone?" I hunched over picturing age spots all over my hands in only partially mock horror.

Lucia swatted my arm with a laugh. "Crone doesn't mean what it used to. It's taking on new form as older women are claiming the title for themselves. It's a sign of wisdom, or of being an elder."

I groaned. "I'm not ready to be called an elder yet." Then a thought occurred to me. "Wait, if I'm officially in menopause, the hot flashes will stop, right? Does that mean the visions will, too?" I noticed a tiny kernel of sadness at the thought.

"I'm afraid we're in uncharted territory here, so I can't say with certainty. A small percentage of women experience hot flashes throughout the rest of their lives."

"The rest of their lives?" I asked in genuine horror.

Lucia quickly added, "I don't know if that will be the case for you, but as the visions just recently began, I'm assuming they, at least, will continue." She closed her eyes for a minute, as if listening to a sound or a voice she alone could hear. When she opened her eyes, there was a twinkle in them.

"It may interest you to know, my mom had psychic abilities and found her insights to be quite useful and quite lucrative. Many called her a modern mystic." A term I would also apply to Lucia. "She was hosting salons on spiritual topics in the fifties in Santa Fe. At the time, it wasn't widely accepted for the average middle-class woman to host discussions on topics viewed as occult. But when the sixties rolled around, Mom became well known in the Santa Fe area as a consultant on all things spiritual." She looked wistful. "I thrived on all Mom taught me and had many animal and spirit friends I talked with as a child."

She sipped her whiskey tea serenely, and I wondered if she was seeing any of those friends over her teacup now. Her face lit up as a thought came to her. "Speaking of moms, have you asked your mom about the visions? Maybe her experience has been similar."

"My mom?" I tried to envision her talking about anything so out of the ordinary.

"Yes. These gifts frequently run in families," she said.

I snorted at the idea it was a gift, but a glance from Lucia made me swallow my laughter.

"I never thought to ask her. Though, surely it would be something she would mention to her only daughter. Right?"

Lucia innocently asked, "So, I can presume you're planning to talk with your own daughters about this?"

While I thought Bailey and Izzy would be more open to the idea than my mom would be, I didn't know how I would broach the subject with any of them. Since that felt far too overwhelming to contemplate, I did the only logical thing. I dodged the question and redirected the conversation to her mom's experience.

"Lucrative sounds good to me. If I'm going to have these insights, I wish they could be more useful."

"You know the old adage. Be careful what you wish for."

A tingle of energy shot down my spine.

CHAPTER FOUR

It wasn't completely dark in the alley behind Past Present Antiques, but it soon would be. He'd practiced for a few nights in his yard to perfect his aim with the slingshot he'd bought online: a small but effective weapon he'd been able to conceal easily inside his jacket. He'd lived in this town long enough to know it would take time for the damaged light to be reported and replaced.

He took careful aim from a spot in a shadow cast by a brick chimney on the other side of the alley in case someone in one of the apartments above the shops was awake. He felt a moment of pride that it took only one shot to dispense with the single security light at the entrance to the alley. The sound of breaking glass was minimal, but he lingered in the shadows a bit longer to be sure no one had noticed.

Holding his breath in the darkness, he felt a familiar anger rise within him. None of this should have been necessary.

After he'd found Margaret's letter among his aunt's things, but not the music book it referred to, he'd been discouraged. He'd tried to imagine what she might have done with it or someone she might have given it to. He knew his mom didn't have it, but he'd thought about his Aunt Mabel's neighbor. She had died not long before his aunt and they'd been close friends for years. He used to run between their houses as a child. The two women had shared everything: family problems, gossip, recipes, and books. He'd remembered how they'd both loved to read and that his aunt's neighbor loved to play the piano. At Christmastime she would play carols and they would all sing along. When he'd casually asked his mom a few questions about her recently, she'd mentioned the neighbor had been a faithful library volunteer, which had given him a glimmer of hope. It had meant it was possible she'd donated her books to the library.

So, he'd started going to the used book sales they had, casually browsing for books that might be old enough, checking the first few pages for Margaret's name, only to be disappointed every time. It was at one of those sales he'd realized the small-town atmosphere was working against him once more.

As a child, he hadn't been aware of how much people knew about each other in a small community. He hadn't yet discovered how helpful or hurtful everyone knowing each other could be. As soon as he got to middle school, he began to learn. When he moved back as an adult, people thought they knew everything they needed to know about him and his mom and their family's long history in Fredericksburg. He'd thought he could return as the man he'd become and be valued for the career he'd built. Maybe to some he was, but very few, it seemed. Others, especially the ones whose own families had a long history here, would only ever see him through his connection to the past, a connection he had dared believe he'd be able to escape.

Then he'd watched the people of this town steal his dreams yet again. Standing between rows of shelves in the library's lobby at a recent book sale, he'd seen Jane Harper arrive. Knowing she owned Past Present and that one of her specialties was rare books, her arrival had piqued his interest. He'd wandered casually closer to the information desk she'd stopped at, while remaining out of sight behind the shelves. He worried she would recognize him and so, didn't want to draw her attention, but he'd wanted to listen to what she said.

What he'd heard had made him want to scream in frustration. She'd strolled right in and asked for a box of books that had been left at the desk for her by Sophie Grace, her friend who worked at the library. Who else would a librarian have given potentially valuable old books to but her friend who deals in rare books? To hell with everyone else. That's all it took, the right connections. The volunteer at the desk had handed it right over, along with all his plans for the future.

They'd left him with no choice. He'd had to come up with Plan B.

CHAPTER FIVE

M y conversation with Lucia prompted me to reach out to my mom the next day. I didn't have any idea what her reaction would be, but even so, it would be a gross under-statement to say our conversation stunned me.

She answered the phone in her usual cheerful way. "Hello, Livvy! How are you?"

"Hi, Mom. I'm doing well. How're you and Dad?"

We went through the usual check-in about their health and how Dad was driving her crazy since he retired, which was eight years ago. So, by all accounts she should be good and crazy by now.

Once the standard topics had run out, there was a pause, which made her mom-radar kick in.

"Is everything OK, honey? Did you have something you wanted to talk to me about?"

I wondered momentarily if it wasn't more than just mom-radar. I hadn't a clue how to begin, so that's how I began. "There is a question I wanted to ask you, but I'm not sure how to begin."

I could hear her moving around, and then the sound of a door closing. "All right, I'm upstairs in my sewing room with the door closed and I'm sitting down. What is it?" It had taken her years to be able to claim my childhood bedroom for herself and her sewing.

There was apprehension in her voice, so I plunged on, more to allay her fears than to address any of my own. "I'm fine. There's nothing wrong. I wondered—there's something that's been going on, and I wondered if it might be, maybe, genetic or something." Not the most coherent start, I suppose.

"Genetic? Are you sick? Just come out and say it if you are."

"No, I promise you I'm not sick. I didn't mean genetic like that."

"Is there another kind of genetic?"

There was confusion in her voice now and I laughed at the silliness of my hesitations. I decided to lay it out for her. "It's more of an emotional or possibly spiritual genetic trait I'm interested in." I thought that would provoke a response, but instead she was silent, which brought my hesitation back up. "It's nothing weird. Well, that might not be entirely true. It may be a little weird, but not insane or anything." I knew I was rambling, so I stopped abruptly.

"Oh, for heaven's sake, spit it out."

"Sorry." I paused in an attempt to quiet my mind before taking the plunge. "Did you ever have unusual dreams or any kind of visions in relation to perimenopause, menopause, or hot flashes?" I had stumbled over the words and found myself holding my breath when I'd finished and as the silence length-ened between us.

She heaved a deep sigh. "No, I never experienced anything like that." My heart sank in my chest. "But my mother did." My heart fluttered.

"Nonna?" She remained silent, so I gently nudged her. "How come you never said anything about it?"

"Well, it wasn't exactly considered a good thing. There were some who thought she was slightly nutty, including me sometimes." Now her words were tinged with regret. "But I came to appreciate it later."

I could tell there was more to this than she was saying. "What happened? Please tell me." There was another pause when I guess she was wondering how much to tell me. "Please, I need to know."

"It was all such a long time ago. No one talked about menopause then. I don't think anyone used the term per-imenopause at the time. All I knew was my mom began to change when I was in my late teens and early twenties. She had always been passionate and even hot-tempered at times. We'd written it off to her Italian heritage, but this was something more."

Thanks to my parents, my brother and I were a mixture of the passionate natures of Italians, through my mom's side of the family, and the Irish through the Wildes on my dad's side. It had its benefits, but also its downsides.

"She had mood swings and insomnia and when she did sleep, she would regularly wake from dreams crying. Dad had no idea what was going on. So, as was common for men of his generation, he tried to ignore it. Their generation didn't talk about emotional things very often. And we thought that was all there was to it, emotional changes, but then . . ." her words trailed off.

"Then what?"

Another sigh. "Strange things started to occur. The phone would ring, and she would pick up the phone and greet the person by name. This was long before there was caller ID, so there was no way she could've known who it was. It was small things like that. Thinking of a friend she hadn't seen in a while and the next day running into them."

Hearing her echo the words I had spoken to Lucia raised goosebumps on my arms.

Her tone was deeper and quieter when she spoke again. "Then on the morning of November twenty-second, nineteen sixty-three, she woke up in hysterics."

Everyone in my family understood the significance of that date. My goosebumps multiplied.

"Dad called me because he couldn't calm her down and he needed to leave for work. It was when we still lived in Haddonfield not far from them, so I got a neighbor to stay with your brother and went over there so Dad could leave.

"It was around nine when I arrived. His expression was grim when he met me at the door. There was fear in his eyes, and I had never seen my dad afraid. He said, 'She keeps going on and on about President Kennedy being dead. I can't convince her he's alive.' He'd tried to get her to watch the news to prove Kennedy was alive, but it had made her sob more."

She grew quiet, reliving the scene. "I told him I would see what I could do, and he left. The first thing I did was put on a pot of coffee. You know how Mom loved coffee and Dad didn't have a clue how to make it himself. I thought the smell of it might calm her down. I went upstairs to their bedroom and found her lying across the bed, still weeping. I sat with her and rubbed her back, like she'd done for me so often. I just kept handing her tissues and letting her cry." Her voice cracked with emotion. "Eventually, she quieted, and I told her I had to go down to check on the coffee and asked if she'd like to come down with me and have a cup. That got her attention. So, we went downstairs arm in arm. I remember we moved slowly. It's funny the things you remember."

I swear I could hear her smile through the phone.

"Then what did you do?" I prompted.

"We sat together at the kitchen table, not talking. Sipping our coffee. After a few minutes, her eyes rested on mine and she said, 'I'm not crazy, Carolina.'"

My mom's name is Caroline, but Nonna had always called her by the Italian version of the name, which is pronounced "Caroleena." She told her the name meant strength. Nonna told me repeatedly all Italian women are strong. The memories of her insistent words helped me immeasurably after Nate died.

Now, a part of me wonders if Nonna told me that repeatedly for a reason she'd never revealed.

Mom continued, "I took her hand and told her, 'I know you're not, Mom, but help us understand what's going on.' That's when she told me all about the visions and dreams she'd been having for years. She'd never shared so much about herself with me before. She'd lost her own mother when she was twelve, so she had no way of knowing if what she was going through was normal or hereditary or a mental illness. She said all she knew was it was connected to the change. That's what they called it."

She paused for a breath. "When she was a girl, she had overheard whispered stories between her older relatives about a great grandmother who was deemed the fortune teller in their Italian village. She said they'd talked about it with awe and wariness, but she didn't know anything more about it. Finally, she looked at me tearfully and said, 'I dreamed President Kennedy had been shot. When I woke, I knew it was true. I think it will be soon.'"

My goosebumps had goosebumps by now.

"I had absolutely no idea what to say. I adored Kennedy. I can't tell you how many times afterward I wished I'd called someone, had tried to warn him somehow, but they wouldn't have listened to me, or might have thought I was a lunatic. All I could say was I prayed in this instance her dream was wrong."

We sat in silence again, lost in our own thoughts.

Kennedy's assassination was two years before I was born, but I learned all about it from my father. He was devastated when each of the Kennedy brothers was assassinated. He wouldn't

hear a bad word about either of them, and had a secret fascination with theories about their deaths. JFK's murder was an
event that had a tremendous impact on our family, and yet, I'd
never been told this part of the story. All I'd heard was Mom had
been at her parents' house when his death had been reported.

Now that I considered it, all the family stories about that day
came from my father. My mom had almost never chimed in.

"How come you and Dad never told us about this? With his
obsession about the Kennedys and their assassinations, he must
have been fascinated by Nonna's story."

When she responded it was in a whisper. "I never told him."

"What? He doesn't know even now? How could you never
have told him?"

"Oh, Liv." Her voice was choked. "You don't understand
what it was like. The whole thing was so devastating and con-
fusing. After Mom and I talked, I called Dad and told him she
was calmer now. He asked if I could stay with her. So, she and I
worked on some sewing together all morning. We were finishing
up lunch when the phone rang around one forty-five. I thought
it might be Dad. I answered it and there was a frantic woman
on the other end. It was Mom's neighbor. The words she was
screaming didn't register at first, but then they sank in. Kennedy
had been shot. Before I even told her, Mom had tears running
down her cheeks, though she was calmer than she'd been earlier.
There was apparently something calming in the confirmation
of what she had dreamed, and she had sort of been given a head
start on the grief. Dad came home a short while later, surprised

to find her so subdued. We talked for a bit, but I had to get home. Your dad had already called in tears to say he was on his way home. I left them in front of the television watching the news. The whole day was such a blur, so filled with anguish, I didn't have the words or strength to tell Ed about my morning. I called Dad that night to see how Mom was and he swore me to secrecy. He was afraid the neighbors would say she was a witch."

I pictured the wariness I'd seen on Sophie's face for just helping her find a phone.

"So, I kept my promise to him. Mom and I talked about it once after Dad passed, but I've never told the story to anyone else. Until today."

I wondered how poor Nonna must have felt that morning when she woke knowing what the day held.

We fell into another silence, alone with our thoughts together. Silence was becoming a participant in the conversation.

"I'm not sure what to make of all this," I said with a touch of despair. "If only I'd been able to talk with Nonna about it. Did she ever try to make use of her gift, her visions, whatever you want to call them? Did she have them for the rest of her life?"

"In their neighborhood in south Jersey? What on earth would she have done with them? It was a strictly blue-collar part of Haddonfield. People weren't interested in visions and fortune telling. They were trying to make a living. No, she mostly kept it to herself other than to help neighbors from time to time."

"Help them how?"

"She would say, 'Do you want some sage advice?' and if they said yes, she would use her insights to help them in small ways without them ever realizing the source of the advice. She did develop a reputation in her neighborhood for being able to find lost things, pets, keys—even a wedding ring one time." She paused, lost in her memories again. "But after she and Dad moved, I didn't hear any more about it. I know it did stay with her, though, because she always knew it was me when I called." She sniffed.

"I'm sorry. I didn't mean to bring up sad memories."

"There's no need to be sorry. They're mostly wonderful memories. I just still miss her more often than you might think."

"I know exactly what you mean."

"Oh. Of course, you do, honey. I—"

I cut her off. "It's OK. I only meant I understand missing someone. It can sneak up on you in the most unexpected situations. You're standing in the grocery store holding a box of the cereal they liked, or you catch a whiff of the shampoo they used, and you're lost in a memory of them. Missing them like crazy."

"They say the grief lessens with time and in most ways it does, but it seems to me missing them never really goes away," she said.

"The intensity of it has lessened a little, but no, it hasn't gone away, and it hasn't gone away for the girls either."

After that we veered off into updates on how Izzy and Bailey were doing, which filled up another quarter of an hour. Before we hung up, I said quietly, "You should tell Dad."

"I know." She sighed heavily, said goodbye, and hung up.

CHAPTER SIX

There were days when Izzy felt the loss of her father more strongly. It was so hard to resist the urge to drop everything and run to Blacksburg to see her when she was having one of those days. In general, she always acted like she had it all together, and most of the time she did, but there were moments when I could see through the façade.

"You're up early. Everything all right?" I asked when she called unexpectedly Friday morning. I knew she didn't have any morning classes to cause her to be up earlier than nine.

"Yeah, I'm fine," Izzy said. She was not as animated as she usually was.

"You sound sad," I said.

Both the girls missed their dad terribly, but for Izzy, who was the more sensitive of the two, the grief was still very near the surface. She didn't like to talk about it, but sometimes she needed to.

She was quiet for a few breaths before speaking, and when she did, her voice trembled slightly. "I'm OK. It's just that I don't get to be around people who knew Dad very often anymore."

My heart broke wide open. I had my friends to talk to, who all knew Nate and me as a couple. It had never occurred to me the girls wouldn't be around people who knew their dad once they were in college and moved away from Fredericksburg.

We each cried a little, and I wished with every fiber of my being that I could hug her. She said she could feel it.

She was quiet when she spoke again. "Tell me the story of how you and Dad met."

I almost dismissed the request because she'd heard the tale many times. Instead, I smiled and said, "Of course, sweetie." After all, it was one of my favorite stories.

"You know how in the movies there's always a perfect meet-cute?" I asked.

"Uh-huh."

"Ours was more like a meet-profane or a meet-messy."

There was a quiet giggle from Izzy.

"Whatever you want to call it, it definitely didn't start out cute." I smiled to myself at the memory. "It was August thirty-first, nineteen ninety-five, and I was at an O's game with a friend. It was the year Cal Ripken broke Lou Gehrig's record for most consecutive games played."

Despite spending most of my youth in south Jersey, I was born in Baltimore. My dad and his whole family were born and raised there. It was a big deal when he fell in love with a girl from New Jersey when he was in college. She had tried to make it a go of it in Baltimore, but the city never felt like home to her. So, when I was three, we moved to Haddonfield, near Grandpa and

Nonna, and when I was in third grade, Mom and Dad bought a house in a small community in the Pine Barrens called Medford Lakes.

Even with its proximity to Philadelphia, where Dad worked, he never became a Phillies fan. Instead, we spent many summer Saturdays and Sundays driving to and from Baltimore to visit family and to see an O's game. Mom said it was the least she could do, since he'd relocated for her. I loved those hot days at the ballpark with my dad. It made me a lifelong baseball fan and, eventually, led me to Nate.

"I had gone to use the bathroom and get another beer in the top of the sixth inning. Beer in hand, I was rushing to make it to our seats before the bottom of the inning. Your dad—"

Izzy interrupted. "You don't have to keep calling him 'your dad.' It's OK for you to call him Nate, Mom."

I had to wipe away tears before continuing. "Nate was walking in the opposite direction and wasn't watching where he was going. He and a buddy were laughing about something. In my mind they were just two of the many guys at the ballpark who go to get drunk, loud, and obnoxious."

"Which you never do, right?"

"Certainly not," I said. "So, I shifted my trajectory to the right to go around them as they neared—but I didn't shift enough. They were apparently reenacting some spectacular catch. I saw Nate's arm swing out in front of me in time to avoid getting hit right in the head, but the Matrix-like maneuver I had to do to avoid being hit meant half of my beer spilled down the front of my shirt and shorts. It was a hot day, but it was one cold beer. Hence the steady stream of obscenities that followed."

"I shouted at him, 'You stupid jerk! Why don't you watch the fucking fuck where you're going, ass-wipe—'"

"Mom!" Izzy said in mock astonishment.

"Hey, Nate would always say how impressed he'd been because some of the words I'd used were new to him," I said. Izzy giggled more genuinely now, and I added, "I always loved that my creative profanity was a source of pride for him. He said it was the first time he'd ever been called an ass-wipe and a fuck-tart in the same breath."

I described the moment I'd finally stopped ranting long enough to see he looked genuinely sorry and slightly alarmed. "That's when I noticed how incredibly cute he was, especially the way his curls spilled out from under his baseball cap."

"And that's when you knew, right?" Izzy asked.

"Well, it's at least when I started paying attention to what was going on," I said.

"And you were thirty when you met?" she asked.

"Yes, and Nate was thirty-three."

"How did it feel when you knew? I don't mean did it make you feel happy, but how did you recognize the feeling that he was the one?"

"That's a good question. I've never thought about it. I guess I just realized I hadn't felt anything like it before." I paused for dramatic effect. "And I had a lot to compare it to, since I had dated a lot of guys before Nate—and I mean a lot."

"Yeah, right," she laughed. She knew I'd had a couple semi-serious relationships prior to meeting her dad, but nothing that could compare to what we had.

I told her the whole story, how he'd convinced me to let him buy me a new beer and some dry clothes. How we spent the rest of the time talking rather than watching much of the game.

"I didn't even mind missing our go-ahead run in the bottom of the sixth. And I loved it when we both stopped in mid-conversation to lament the A's two runs in the top of the ninth. I loved so many things about those last three-and-a-half innings." I ended with a sigh. It was part comfort and part torture to have these conversations with Izzy, but I would never tell her that.

"You know, even though I didn't really believe in signs when we met, I still thought it was a sign that his last name was Brown when the Orioles had formerly been the Browns. Baseball fans are a superstitious bunch."

"It always comes back to baseball," she mock-groaned. "Do you believe in signs now?"

I hesitated briefly and said, "I'm starting to."

CHAPTER SEVEN

L ater in the afternoon, I was preparing for our Monthly and feeling grumpy. My grumpiness reminded me of the first time I had introduced any of my friends to G.G. It was the one time Hannah had arrived early, and no, Hannah isn't a foolish euphemism for my period. Hannah is one of the five ladies I get together with on the second Friday of every month for what we affectionately call our Monthly.

It was a few years ago. She'd arrived at my place almost an hour early, way before I would even have been expecting Claire, who was always the first to arrive. I was afraid she was dying, because she was so serious when she walked in and said, "I need to talk to you."

We'd sat on the couch together, hitting the wine earlier than usual. I was still a bit nervous when she'd faced me and said, "I'm just gonna say this straight out. I've been worried about you for a while now. You've been short-tempered and honestly, kind of bitchy, and not as much fun to be around. I thought it might be because you haven't had sex since Nate died, but now I think

I understand." She'd paused for a beat. "Are you going through the fucking change?"

Laughing, I said, "What are you, a hundred years old? Nobody calls it that anymore."

"Well, that's what they should call it because I feel like a changeling! You have to help me figure this out."

My laughter had faded. "I know exactly what you mean. I'm sorry I've been so grumpy. There are times when *I* don't even like being around me. I can't tell you how often I feel like I'm possessed and someone else is speaking instead of me. I wouldn't be surprised if my head started spinning around! It's like I don't recognize myself anymore. I look in the mirror and wonder, who is that grumpy gal? In fact, I've started calling her that whenever I'm particularly irritable. I say, 'Grumpy Gal's visiting.' Now I just call her G.G."

Hannah had assumed a serious demeanor and raised her glass. "To G.G."

"To G.G." Our glasses connected with a satisfying chime. I took a sip and said, "The only blessing I've been able to find in Nate's death at fifty is at least he didn't have to meet G.G." After another sip of wine, I said, "I'm glad you brought it up."

"Yeah, I bet," she laughed.

"Seriously. I knew I'd been snapping at people, even the girls have mentioned it. Bailey thought I was mad at her last week on the phone, when it was just G.G."

"They'll understand one day." Hannah had sighed and smiled at the same time.

"I don't seem to be able to do anything about it. One minute I'm my normal self—at least my new normal self—and the next I'm G.G."

My new normal, which meant a more sedate version of myself since Nate's death, had been the topic of previous Monthlies. Now, not only was I no longer as wild as my name might indicate, but I was also short-tempered, along with sleep-deprived and sweaty. A lovely combination.

The more we'd talked, the more we'd realized how little either of us knew about menopause. Being the oldest in our group, we were the first to deal with it. You might think middle-aged, intelligent women would be aware of the signs and symptoms of menopause, but it's not a subject people want to discuss in detail, not even doctors.

"And what the hell is perimenopause?" Hannah had asked. "I didn't even know there was another part to the process that was called anything other than menopause. I thought that one word encapsulated the whole process."

I laughed half-heartedly. "I've started calling it permanentpause because I swear, I had to put a permanent pause on everything I used to enjoy doing, on who I used to be. I was changing into someone else without my permission. It was like Invasion of the Body Snatchers, and the woman who was emerging from the pod was not who I wanted to be." I had dropped my gaze, before adding, "And I was afraid I wasn't the woman my friends wanted to hang out with anymore, either."

Hannah had reached out and held my hand. "We'd never give up on you," she said. "No matter how bitchy you got." We'd laughed, but we'd both known she meant it.

"I felt so clueless when the whole thing started," I said. "It wasn't until I started having hot flashes a hundred times a day that I finally started to catch on."

"And it's not just the heat and sweating either. At first, it felt like I was having anxiety attacks," Hannah said.

"Oh my gosh, yes. It's just like an anxiety attack when it begins. It makes me feel trapped in my own skin. It's what I would guess a heart attack must feel like, except it happens a hundred times a day." Hannah had cocked an eyebrow at me. "All right, maybe only ninety-nine, and I almost always have them when it's the most inconvenient."

"Yes," Hannah exclaimed. "They almost never kick in when I'm cold and have to pull on socks to warm my frozen toes. Instead, it's when I'm in the checkout line at the grocery store, or sitting at a table in a restaurant, or as soon as I snuggle under the covers at night, or worst of all, when I'm talking to a handsome man."

Hannah liked to talk to handsome men. She was married but was still the unapologetic flirt of our group.

"Oh, that's my favorite one," I said, my eyes rolling to the ceiling. I still hadn't started dating since becoming a widow. Whenever I thought about it what went through my mind was, "*who'll be able to compete with the love of my life?*" But it didn't mean I didn't appreciate an attractive man. "It's not bad enough that after the age of fifty most men tend to write us off as potential partners, as opposed to some forty-year-old with no gray in her hair and no back-fat—but then if they do take an interest, I break into a sweat and find myself with rosy cheeks and sweat beading on my upper lip and rolling down my back."

Hannah had raised her glass again and with a straight face said, "There's nothing sexier than a sweaty upper lip."

After Hannah and I talked that first time, things got a bit easier. Giving my perimenopause personality her own name and, in a way, celebrating her, took some of the power away from her. Now when I'm unusually grumpy, I stop and remind myself it's only G.G. It gave me a way to laugh at myself and not take it all too seriously and, for better or worse, she also gives my friends a way to point out when I'm being a little, or a lot, bitchy.

Our Monthlies are always potluck affairs. We rotate hosting duties, mostly so we can each be assured a reason to thoroughly clean our homes every six months. It's the same group every time: Sophie, Jane, Claire, Mary, Hannah, and me. We cover the matrimonial spectrum from married, to divorced, to never married, to widowed. Between us we have eight children, two dogs, three cats, one snake (not including ex-husbands), one ongoing extramarital affair, and four therapists (some of us have the same one). Obviously, we have a lot to talk about every month.

It was April, my turn to host. The host gets to choose the main course, and everyone chimes in using our potluck app (which Izzy hooked me up with) regarding the side dish, appetizer, or dessert they will bring. It's a given a couple people will bring wine, or every now and then a specialty drink. We enjoy making up fun, mashup names for drinks. Mary likes to experiment with cocktails from time to time, particularly in the summer, and we all suggest creative, usually inappropriate, names for them.

She made up a drink when Nate and I were celebrating our fifteenth anniversary. Let's just say it was an acquired taste. It was a riff on a cocktail called Penicillin. Her version was a combination of scotch (it was practically all Nate would drink), a dash of lemon and lime juice (for those sour moments in a relationship), honey (for the sweet times), and a tiny splash of absinthe (to keep things lively!). Nate loved it. In true Brangelina style Mary christened it the Late for Liv and Nate, and since we got married later in life than was normal at the time and so had kids later too.

The name wasn't so funny anymore after Nate died.

I've always wondered why we use the words we do for death. The "late" Nathan Brown. It's hard to imagine he's late for anything now. Or "passed away." What is that supposed to mean? It sounds so gentle, like he slowly faded away. Yet there was nothing gentle about it when it happened, or afterwards.

I keep a bottle of absinthe tucked away in a cabinet and every year on the second Friday in February, we make Lates and drink a toast to Nate. It's no contest. I have the best friends in the world.

After Nate's car accident I moved from our somewhat historic home (meaning a home in need of constant upkeep and improvements) in downtown Fredericksburg to the renovated townhouse I'm in now on Sophia Street. Sophie likes to say I chose the location as a tribute to her because of the name of the street and because she works at the library next door. But the weird thing about Sophia Street is that around here it is pronounced So-f-eye-a. It's thought to be named in honor of King George II's sister Sophia, but it still doesn't explain the pronunciation.

The building I live in, Mary Washington Square, had been the original hospital here in town, named after George Washington's mother. There are rumors the place has ghosts lingering from its days as a hospital, but I've been here going on three years now and I haven't witnessed any. No confirmed sightings at least.

The people who live here are all either middle-aged professionals like me or retired folks. There aren't any families with young children. Some are rentals and others are owned by the people who live in them. They are all well-appointed, meaning expensive. But they offered the trifecta of what I was searching for: renovated, near the river, and downtown.

I couldn't bring myself to leave the historic district, but I couldn't keep up with the repairs an older home requires, either. I gave it my best effort after Nate died, but once Izzy went off to college, it was time. Still, it was difficult for all of us to give up the home and all the memories tied up in it.

Izzy, Bailey, and I had some long heart-to-heart conversations before I put it on the market. In the end we all decided it might be time for a new beginning, which for me needed to include a new space. I couldn't leave it all behind, however. I took a small piece of it with me. I blamed Jimmy Stewart.

You know the round finial at the bottom of the banister in *It's a Wonderful Life*, the one that came off in George Bailey's hand every time he came down the stairs? Nate and I watched the movie the first Christmas we celebrated in the house. Afterward, we unscrewed the finial on our banister so it would come loose. It was a reminder to stay focused on what truly matters, on what makes a person rich. I couldn't leave it behind. I knew I would continue to need it as a reminder. It now sits in a basket on the table beside my front door, where my friends smile and touch it with gentleness when they enter or leave.

For April, I went with a springtime-in-Fredericksburg theme. It's my favorite month around here because the bald eagles are out in force by then and can be seen daily along the Rappahannock River, hunting for shad traveling upstream.

One year the water level was unusually low during the April shad run. With the fish so plentiful and the water so low, the water looked like it was boiling when their bodies broke the surface as they ran the gauntlet of fishermen, rapids, ospreys, and eagles on their way upstream. This year it was the opposite. We'd had a couple rainy weeks, and the water level was high.

While April showers bring May flowers, in a city on a river, spring showers can bring high waters and floods too. On one of my walks earlier in the week, I'd noticed the water gauge on the opposite bank along Fall Hill Avenue was on the border between the yellow level, meaning stay off the river, and the red level, indicating life-threatening conditions.

I shivered and tried to shake off the memory of rushing water.

I would have chosen shad for our April main course, but they are notoriously difficult to eat due to the profusion of hard-to-remove bones. Instead, I went with a simple recipe for roasted red snapper I found in a cookbook.

Claire arrived as I was rearranging things in the fridge to hide the casserole I'd made as my backup dish in case the fish was a disaster. She let herself in, as my friends always do. Though more than once Sophie had entered without knocking when I wasn't expecting her and scared the daylights out of me. She told me it was my own fault for not locking my door.

"You're even earlier than usual," I said as Claire came in and set a bowl of rice she'd prepared on the kitchen counter. There were a handful of fuchsia flowers arranged nicely on top of the rice.

"I was over at the Mary Washington House in the garden for their annual spring gardening program. That's where the redbud flowers came from," Claire said.

"We're not supposed to eat them, are we?"

She laughed. "Of course you are. They're harmless and add a touch of sweetness."

She removed the light coat she was wearing. On the navy-blue cardigan underneath was her name tag from her job at the James

Monroe Museum. The museum employees in town tried to support each other's events when they could.

She'd started working at JMM on weekends twice a month when her kids were preteens. She'd said they needed the extra income, but her husband Jonathan had a good, executive-level position with a government contractor in Northern Virginia. So, I think she just wanted to have some regular time away from her daughters. Heaven knows all parents can use quality time away from their kids occasionally. When they were in high school, she started picking up extra hours during the week. Now, she has a regular schedule there two days a week and two Sundays a month.

She took off the name tag and put it in her purse and went back down the hall to hang her coat and purse in the closet. Claire was always put-together, organized, and neat, and her short blonde bob almost never had a hair out of place. "Where's the wine?" She was also a lush.

"I hadn't put it out yet," I said. I pulled two bottles of white wine, one Chardonnay and one a dry Riesling, from the fridge and handed them to Claire, who placed them on the counter beside the wine glasses I'd set out.

"Let's see," she said as she perused the selection of wine glasses. "Which one should I choose this time?" She chose a hand-painted one I'd bought at a local craft show last year. "I always like having dinner at your place. Having different glasses means we don't need to put charms on them to remember whose is whose." This was her nice way of saying she appreciated my eclectic style. Claire's wine glasses all matched.

She selected the Riesling and opened it, pouring us each some. She handed me a glass with a purple stem she'd selected for me, then sipped from her glass.

"I don't like sweet Rieslings, but this is nice and dry," she said.

I enjoyed a sip of it myself and asked, "How are Emma and Joy?"

"They're doing well. It hasn't really sunk in yet that Joy's freshman year at Mason is ending soon."

"It's amazing how fast it goes by. I can't wrap my head around the idea that Izzy will graduate next year."

"I can't even think about it," said Claire. "I'm driving to Charlottesville in the morning to spend the day with Emma."

"Oh, that'll be wonderful. Has she finalized her plans for grad school?"

"Oh, you know Emmaline, she leaves everything to the last minute. It's part of what we'll be doing tomorrow, making some plans. I might have to leave early tonight so I can get a decent night's sleep." Claire reserved Emma's full name for times when she was worried about something she was doing.

"You mean so you won't be hungover for tomorrow," I laughed.

"She does pick up on those things."

"Yes, because she learned through experience and from an expert," I said. "Jonathan's told us about your wild child days, so that apple didn't fall far from the tree."

She laughed. "You should know by now you can't trust everything Jonathan tells you."

He and Claire got together in college, and he'd shared some stories about her from their college days that had surprised us, at least until we had gotten to know her better. Over the years she'd revealed more of her wild side at our Monthlies.

"How's he enjoying working from home more often?"

Claire perked up. "He loves it. It's only one or two days a week, but anything that reduces the number of hours he spends slogging his way up ninety-five is helpful."

"Amen," I said. "I hated it. It was soul-sucking."

Many people are employed by government contractors around here, or by the federal government, and commute from Fredericksburg to Northern Virginia or D.C. The rush hour traffic on Interstate 95 can easily transform a one-hour drive into three.

"Yup, soul-sucking, just like a Dementor," Claire said.

"Geez, we're talking about sucking already?" said Hannah, whom we hadn't heard come in. "I haven't even had a drink yet." She was grinning and carrying a couple bottles of wine.

If you can count on Claire to be the first to arrive, Hannah can be counted on to always bring a bottle of wine or two. Our dinners are not exactly dry affairs, thank God.

CHAPTER EIGHT

"Liv, the snapper was delicious." Jane raved as I carried empty plates to the sink.

"And it wasn't even your backup dish, was it?" asked Sophie, laughing.

Halfway to the table from the kitchen, my jaw dropped at her words. "My backup dish?"

They all laughed until they almost fell off their chairs. I couldn't help but laugh with them, plus there had been plenty of wine.

"You didn't honestly think it was a secret, did you?" Sophie asked.

"Come on," Claire said. "When do we ever see extra food in your refrigerator when the girls aren't home? Yet, every time I arrive for a Monthly, there's always a mysterious casserole dish covered with foil neatly tucked away in the fridge."

"Hey, we were grateful when we discovered it. It meant we had a better shot at a decent meal when you were hosting," said Jane. She laughed as she said it, but with gentleness. She's an amazing cook and had tried to help me improve my cooking skills over the years, with moderate success. "I admit I was concerned when I saw you were going to be cooking fish, since we haven't had much luck with it in our lessons in the past, but you did a great job. Where'd you get the recipe?"

I returned to the kitchen and from behind my regular cookbooks pulled out a copy of *Seafood Cooking for Dummies*. Hiding it behind me, I grabbed my wine glass and raised it into the air. "You can thank the dummies!"

As they all raised their glasses and their eyebrows, I brandished the book in front of them. Sophie might have peed her pants a little we laughed so hard.

It happens to some of us at this age. Don't laugh too hard or sneeze too big, or there might be an unwelcome surprise. It's just the way it is as we are all either moving through or approaching perimenopause and menopause, and all the uninvited and unwelcome changes.

"Stop. I can't breathe," Jane moaned. "Tell me that's not where you found the recipe. I will consider myself a complete failure if dummies could teach you and I couldn't."

"I'm afraid it says more about me than you." I leaned over to Sophie, who was wiping away tears. "Water leaking out anywhere else?" I asked, which only led to further gasping for air.

That's generally how most of our gatherings go, filled with enough laughter and friendship to carry us through until next month. Our dinners and their laughter have been a lifesaver for more than one of us over the years.

Sophie dragged herself up and hobbled and laughed all the way to the bathroom.

Things had settled down somewhat when she reappeared and she said, "I'm telling you, I need to get to the doctor and talk to her about this. I know they try to convince us those Poise things are sexy in the TV ads, but hell, no. I'm not ready to be poised."

"Is it getting worse?" Hannah asked. "For me it got worse before it started to get better."

The topic of our bodies changing without our consent was a common theme at our dinners. It's a part of why we limited the invitation list, and why husbands, partners, and kids were banned from the home of whoever is hosting or were at least banished to their man caves and bedrooms. We've found we all need a safe space to talk. Luckily, we seemed to cycle through major life challenges at slightly different times, so, we'd gotten rather good at helping each other navigate them. This was one we all had to deal with, and we'd found it wasn't only me and Hannah who didn't have a lot of information going into it.

After I'd introduced Hannah to G.G. we'd taken to whispering at our Monthlies about what we were going through. We found at first, even among our closest friends, we were embarrassed to talk about it. We hadn't been aware we were being secretive until Mary called us on it at dinner one Friday, asking what Hannah and I were discussing that the rest of them couldn't be in on.

Mary's a no-bullshit, straightforward person. We have yet to discover a topic she won't broach or anything she isn't willing to say about someone as long as she can put a "Bless her/his heart" at the end of it. She's the one who taught me southern women can swear as creatively as northern ones. "Mother Trucker" being one of my personal favorites.

Hannah and I ended up being grateful to Mary for calling us out on our whispering. Once we started talking about it openly, we found out Jane was experiencing some of the same symptoms.

It wasn't long before our hot flashes, night sweats, insomnia, sadly lowered libidos, weight gain, laughter-induced peeing, and numerous other glamorous symptoms were frequently the topic of conversations, rants, and commiseration. While menopause may not have been a process that brought us closer together with our partners, it had brought us even closer together as friends.

—e&e—

Claire was the first to arrive and the first to leave. She made her excuses about getting up early to go see Emma. There was some general harassment for ducking out early, but I understood when your kids wanted to spend the day with you, there was no way you were going to say no.

The rest of the ladies hung around after dessert for more conversation, laughter, and another glass of wine. Sophie and Mary were the last to leave. I walked them to the door, and when Sophie bent to retrieve her purse from the floor, she swore.

"What's the matter?" Mary asked.

"I brought a couple books that were donated to the library. I thought Claire might want to show them to her boss at the museum. I blame Hannah for making me forget. She was talking about Chris when I first came in and I threw my stuff down so I wouldn't miss it. It made me forget all about the books."

Chris was the man Hannah had been having an affair with on and off for a few years now. They were currently in an on-again phase. There was much debate when Hannah was around and when she wasn't, about the need to end the affair. Generally, none of us approved of cheating, especially since a couple of us had been on the receiving end of it at some point in our lives. However, her relationship with her husband Simon was complicated to say the least. They had split up for eight months after he'd been unfaithful, and while they were separated, Hannah had started seeing Chris.

"It serves you right for wanting to hear the gossip," I admonished with a smile.

"Oh, right, and where were you when I came in? Right next to her, drinking in every word." Sophie said.

"Drinking in every drop is more like it," Mary chimed in.

We laughed as Sophie picked up her purse and the paper bag with the books in it. "Will you hang on to these, Liv? I'm sure you'll see Claire again before I will."

"No problem." I reached for the bag. "Why these books in particular?"

Sophie hesitated, "They were part of a bequest one of our oldest volunteers made in her will. I almost included them in a box of books I gave to Jane to go through, but I hung on to these two because they were from the early 1800s. I thought they might have historic value, not just resale value. So, I removed them from the books set aside for the sale to give them to Claire to take to the museum."

"Sounds pretty cool," I said peeking into the bag.

Sophie stopped me, saying, "Don't mess with them. They're a little fragile."

Reluctantly, I pulled my hands away from the edges of the bag. "I'm planning to drop by the museum next week for lunch. I can bring them to her then."

She gingerly handed the bag over to me.

"I promise I will get them to her safely."

"Perfect. Thank you."

They each hugged me and grazed their hands over the finial by the door as they left. The top of it was becoming shiny from all the hands that had given it the same loving farewell.

I leaned against the closed door and sighed. My body began heating up but rather than the normal anxious feeling, I felt instead the hairs rise on the nape of my neck, and a tingling of attentiveness. I dismissed the sensation and returned to the living room in search of my wine glass and finding it, flopped down on the couch, dropping the bag on the floor next to it. I was curious about the books but was more curious whether my wine glass was still cold enough to cool off my forehead.

Sadly, it was not. Hoping it would cool me down from the inside out instead, I raised my glass in silent salute and reluctant surrender to the inner furnace.

CHAPTER NINE

He was glad his hunch had been right. He knew he would set off the alarm when he opened the window in the bathroom and made his escape into the alley, but since the security light hadn't yet been fixed, he'd be hard to spot as he made his way through the alley, down the street, and out of sight before the police arrived.

It'd been a long wait until Jane left for the night at eight o'clock, and he knew he'd need to wait even longer before moving around the store. He'd purposely chosen a Sunday night because there'd be less late-night traffic on Caroline Street, but he waited anyway, just to be sure. He'd prepared for it. He had a burner cell phone for entertainment and to use as an alarm clock in case he fell asleep, and he had a snack to eat after she left. He'd been fasting since the previous day so he wouldn't have to worry about needing to use the bathroom while waiting for her to close up the store. He was no criminal mastermind, but he'd tried to plan for everything—and so far, it had gone smoothly.

It had taken him several trips to the store to find a suitable place to hide. There were two security cameras in the store, so his hiding spot had to be out of the direct line of sight of both cameras. He'd worn different hats, coats, and glasses each time he'd visited to scout out the store. The last thing he'd wanted was for Jane to recognize him or for it to register he kept visiting the store without buying anything, so he'd simply made himself nondescript. It didn't surprise him they hadn't noticed him. He knew how easy it was to be ignored.

He'd known once he was in the store on the evening of the break-in, getting the timing right would be essential. It had to be late enough in the day that the odds of another customer discovering him by accident would be slim. Yet, there had to be other people in the store—otherwise he'd stand out, and she might question whether he had left.

Luck had been on his side for a change. When he'd arrived shortly before five, Jane was the sole employee in the store. The day had cooled off quickly enough that the light gloves he wore weren't out of place. There had been two women browsing near the front windows, and a couple came in not long after he had. He'd hoped they would make a purchase to distract Jane so he could slip into his hiding spot unseen, but they'd only been interested in the jewelry cases. At least that had kept them away from him. The women who'd been browsing at the front when he'd arrived were friends of Jane's. They'd stopped to chat with her on their way out, giving him the opportunity he'd been waiting for. He'd tucked himself quickly away and settled down to wait.

It had been a relief when she'd finally switched off the lights and left. She'd done a lap around the store before leaving but hadn't come near enough to him to cause concern. He'd smiled to himself as he heard her lock the door from the outside of the shop.

She didn't realize what she had, but he did, and it was his ticket out of this place. He had sworn he would never come back, but the job offer had been good with excellent benefits, so against his better judgment, he'd taken it. He hadn't regretted it at first.

Now he would get what he'd come for, sell it for what it was truly worth, and escape for a life of leisure. He wasn't one for the cliché of hiding in the tropics. He had a better plan. It was amazing what you could find on the Internet if you knew the right sites to go to, and it was equally amazing what you could afford in countries dealing with financial difficulties. He had a whole new identity created and would buy a modest home in Greece, surrounded by history, and begin again, just another nondescript American expat.

It was Greece he was thinking of as he gently opened the door to the armoire and crawled out. The space inside it was roomy enough, so he hadn't needed to stay in a terribly uncomfortable position. It was the fact he'd had to remain in one position for so long that had been the issue. Those old armoires could be creaky, so any movement could have made a sound she might have heard and investigated. He'd thought he would need to lie still for an hour or two, but it had taken longer. He'd known all along if it became necessary to change position, he would only be able to make tiny, extremely slow movements. Heaven forbid he'd have an urge to sneeze. It had been his greatest fear in the dusty cabinet, but he'd managed to remain hidden, which was good because try though he might, he hadn't been able to come up with a plausible excuse to give had anyone discovered him. That was the biggest flaw in his plan. He wasn't convinced he would have been prepared to use violence had Jane found him. Luckily for them both, it hadn't proved to be a problem.

He slid to the floor and quickly closed the doors of the armoire, hoping no one was passing by outside—though if someone saw the door move, they would probably chalk it up to a haunting in a town with so many ghost stories. And after all, he had a ghost of sorts with him.

He pulled the letter from the bag hidden beneath his sweatshirt. After reading it for the hundredth time, he tucked it safely away and hungrily ate the granola bar he'd brought along to break his fast. Playing games on the phone entertained him for a while, but eventually he dozed off.

By the time his alarm went off at three a.m., the vibrating phone on his chest having awoken him, he was lying moderately comfortably on the floor, out of sight of the windows and cameras. He stretched and raised his head, cautiously peering through the space between two dressers to see if there was anyone on the street. Once he determined the coast was clear, he crouched low between the aisles of furniture and began to make his way to the locked door that would be the greatest obstacle between him and his goal.

He had to make two stops on his way to the door. He unzipped a pocket on the inside of his dark coat and pulled out a can of black spray paint. Crawling purposefully from aisle to aisle, remaining beneath the height of the dressers, desks, and tables, he arrived at the wall nearest the front door. This was the step involving the most risk, when he would be the most exposed to anyone passing by.

He hesitated as headlights reflected off the shops across the street. The car continued up Charlotte Street without turning onto Caroline, so he seized the opportunity and rose quickly to his feet, pressing his back against the wall directly behind the security camera.

Stretching his arms up on either side of the camera and standing on his toes, he sprayed the lens of the camera with black paint. He'd been careful to make sure his glove was tucked into the sleeve of his jacket so they wouldn't even be able to identify his skin color if they spotted him on the footage for a frame or two. He even thought to catch a drop or two of dripping paint with a bandanna in the other hand. The longer it took the police or Jane to discover the cameras were blacked out, the better, so, why draw their attention to it with paint on the floor?

Dropping to his hands and knees again, he made his way along the path he'd mapped out in his mind hundreds of times to the other security camera. This one pointed at the door of the rare book room. He couldn't have it recording his presence as he worked. Another quick reach from behind, spray, and wipe with the bandanna—and he was ready.

He found he needed to stop to catch his breath. He hadn't realized it would raise his heart rate so much, but the thrill of what he was doing—combined with the risk of being caught—was more intense than he'd imagined.

After allowing his heart rate to slow, he approached the door with the freedom of knowing he couldn't be seen by the cameras, yet still wary of any passersby. There weren't many things in this store of great enough value to keep locked up, other than some jewelry and Jane's rare book collection. A collection which was no doubt the envy of her friend Sophie.

When Sophie had ruined his chance of getting the book legally, and so cheaply, he'd had to regroup. He couldn't take the risk Jane might discover the letters herself, however limited the risk might be. So, he'd planned the break-in meticulously, his frustration with Sophie and Jane serving as his motivation.

He was so sick of the friend-of-a-friend-of-a-friend mentality. They tried to explain it away, saying people simply watched out for one another in small towns. But he knew it wasn't true. They hadn't watched out for him and his mom after his dad died. And why? Because of a betrayal six generations ago that no one even remembered the details of? They remembered the label, though. It was unfathomable to him it could still have made them somehow unworthy of help or kindness.

So, he'd learned to take care of himself and his mom, and really, that's all he was doing now. Once he sold the letters, he would set up a secure account for her to cover her expenses for the rest of her life. He could then invest the rest using his new identity to support himself as well. He doubted they would even hunt for him, since they wouldn't have any idea of the true worth of what he'd stolen—but he wanted to disappear anyway, just in case. It wouldn't be an extravagant life, but that's not what he desired. All he wanted was a place of his own, where people knew nothing about him or his family. It didn't seem like too much to ask.

When he stopped to consider it, there was a certain irony in his own family history leading him to discover the potential existence of the letters. It amazed him how tangled lives and history could become when he finally saw all the pieces in place. How could people in his family tree, people he had never met, have such a big impact on his life? How could a family's legacy stretch so far into the future on the shoulders of their descendants? How could he be so grateful for one relative he had known and so resentful toward another born long before him? These were questions he couldn't dwell on for long, but ones which often haunted him.

He shook off his reverie and checked his watch. A half-hour had passed. He needed to stay focused so he could escape before people started to wake. With so many local residents commuting to jobs in D.C. and Northern Virginia by train and car, the town would be stirring by as early as four a.m. His timing had to be just right. A jogger out on the streets at four might stand out, but a half-hour later would go unnoticed as someone getting in some exercise prior to making the slog on Interstate 95.

At first, he'd worried about how to get in through the locked door to the rare book room. He'd known he didn't have a lot of time to make an elaborate plan and risk someone else buying the book or Jane examining it closely. To be fair, he'd contemplated buying the book and had even searched for it on the shelves one day to see what Jane was asking for it, but he hadn't seen the book on the shelves for sale. He'd been afraid she'd already sold it, but during one of his visits, she'd been on the phone at the counter discussing a book show at which she was going to have a booth. She said she had a box of newly acquired books she thought she'd be able to sell there. Now he could see a sealed box through the window of the book room, and his pulse quickened.

His method of obtaining the code for the door had been primitive, but effective. If the keypad for the security system for the entire building hadn't been in her office, he might have been able to get that code too and save himself some trouble. The one for the book room was the important one, though. Having it would give him time to find the right book. Luckily, this keypad was in a public part of the store, a part of the store with lots of detritus from countless estate sales from various decades. It had been a simple thing to drop an appropriately antiqued pen with a tiny hidden camera on a shelf at the right angle near the end of the day. He'd watched her remotely as she punched in the code and had easily pocketed the pen another day. If someone bought it in the meantime, she might have sold it without being any the wiser.

Without hesitation he typed in the code above the door handle and heard the sweet click of the deadbolt unlocking. He opened the door and slipped inside. From his pocket he drew out his pocketknife and sliced through the tape on the box, being careful not to go too deeply with the blade for fear of damaging the books. If the music book was on top, he didn't want to damage the cover because he could sell it in addition to what was hidden inside. Between the security lighting in the store and the spill from the streetlights, he didn't need to bother with a flashlight.

He began pulling books out while keeping an eye on the street. Most of them were classic novels, but he opened them anyway, flipping through the first few pages hoping to find Margaret's bookplate as an indication he was getting close. He could only guess what size the music book would be. He assumed it had to be larger in height and width than a novel but hoped it wouldn't be much larger or it would be hard to conceal beneath his sweatshirt.

He set the books aside in order, so he could return them to the box in the same way they'd been packed. The longer it took her to realize what his target had been, the better.

As he dug deeper and deeper into the box, he began to feel concerned. He felt excitement course through him when he opened an old copy of *A Christmas Carol* and found his aunt's neighbor's name written inside. At least it proved Jane did have books from her collection. He was on the right track. Yet he could see there were only a few books left.

He reached the last book in the box and flipped through it, though he knew it wasn't the one he'd come here to find. He went through the line of books on the counter again, opening them all one more time hoping to see Margaret's bookplate, or her name written by hand, but he didn't find it in a single book. He frantically scanned the books on the shelves and checked behind counters for more boxes. He looked through the window between the rare book room and Jane's office but didn't see any other boxes.

For a third time he picked up each of the books he'd removed from the box. Sweat beaded on his forehead. He wiped it with his sleeve and checked his watch. He was behind schedule. He needed to pack the books up and escape, but if he escaped without the book, had nothing to show for all his planning, the whole night would be a total loss and could land him in jail for nothing.

He tried to contain his fury as he considered what to do. He had to have something to show for his efforts, so he quickly perused the books from the box one last time. Finally, he selected an old copy of *Pride and Prejudice*, which based on a quick look at the year of publication, was one he thought might bring a decent price from a buyer who didn't ask questions. On impulse, he also set aside the copy of *A Christmas Carol* that had belonged to his aunt's neighbor. It was the one book he felt he had more claim to than Jane did. He placed the rest back in the box in their original order and hurriedly folded the flaps of the box into place. From his inside jacket pocket, he withdrew a roll of packing tape, a precaution he'd thought potentially excessive, and re-taped the box.

He tucked the books beside the letter in the plastic-lined cloth pouch hanging from his neck under his sweatshirt, then closed and locked the door to the rare book room and made his way quickly to the bathroom. He climbed up on the sink, braced himself, lifted the latch, and pulled open the window.

It took only seconds for the alarm to go off, but he was already on the ground. He made his way straight down the space between buildings and stuck to the shadows wherever he could. He had to get down to the river without being seen so he could ditch his jacket and phone in the water. He waited impatiently for one car to pass. Once he could see no one else coming, he ran across Sophia Street and down into the cover of the trees on the riverbank, encountering no one on his way.

He threw the phone as far out into the river as he could, then stuffed his gloves in the pockets of his jacket before taking it off and throwing it into the water after the phone. He watched it begin to drift away with the river's current, then ran up to the road, silently hoping the weight of the can of spray paint in the interior pocket would help the jacket sink quickly.

By the time he got to the sidewalk he had his earbuds in his ears, his hood was up, and he was running swiftly, but not too fast. A jogger out for a morning run. The books, hidden beneath his slightly larger-than-necessary sweatshirt, made a quiet but audible thump as he ran, but surely it wouldn't be loud enough for anyone to notice. The earbuds were for show—he didn't want any music playing, so he could listen for sirens—but even so, after another two blocks, he could barely hear the store's alarm anymore.

CHAPTER TEN

There weren't a lot of other girls named Olivia in my classes growing up in small-town Jersey. I had many days of longing to be a Lisa or a Susan, anything more normal. It took some time for me to appreciate the uniqueness of my name. I started calling myself Liv when I was twelve, in honor of Liv Ullmann, who to my tween self was the height of sophistication. In my teens, Liv Wilde (a distant relation to Oscar, believe it or not) became a name to try to live up to, and I did my damnedest to do just that.

In retrospect, I realized we should have taken my own behavior into consideration before we chose Wilde for Bailey's middle name. I'd overheard her use the phrase "Wilde is my middle name," more than once in her teens. In time, I got past the overly enthusiastic "live up to my name" phase (mostly) and hopefully she has too (mostly), and we each came through it unscathed (mostly).

While Liv Ullmann may only be my self-styled namesake, I recently came across another reason to admire her. Instead of working as diligently as I should one day, I went down an

Internet rabbit hole and discovered an interview with the actress. One section in particular jumped out at me. She said, "What I have always loved most in men is imperfection." She went on to say how things like wrinkles make her love a man more, while women fear men seeing their imperfections. The quote ended with how sad she thought it was that women have a hard time believing a man could love his wife more "because he remembers who she was and sees who she is and thinks, God, isn't that lovely that this happened to her. And be moved by life telling its story there."

As a relatively new single woman, I appreciated the reminder to love a man's imperfections, of which there will no doubt be many if I ever get up the nerve to date.

Sometimes I'm uncertain if I'm single or a widow. Are you both? Is there a line you cross after a specific amount of time when you transition from widow to single? No one offered me a guideline about it in any of the books I eventually read about grief and living beyond it. Whatever I'm officially to be called at this point in my life, besides sweaty, it was the second half of the quote that felt so poignant to me in my life without Nate. With my husband gone, no one will have my younger self as a reference point for thinking, "God, isn't that lovely that this happened to her." Who will be moved "by life telling its story there?" The question keeps me up at night.

It's not the only thing keeping me up at night. Perimenopause-induced insomnia—that's the other thing. They should make women and their partners take a class about the process in their forties. It could save so many relationships, so many people's sanity, and so many dairy cows. (There's no telling how many pints of ice cream I've eaten since this all started. Don't judge. It's a frozen delight which, in the midst of a hot flash, feels like the only possible path to cooling down.) I did mention sanity was an issue during this process, right?

Besides the visions, the insomnia has been the greatest challenge to my sanity. I don't need a ridiculous amount of sleep—with even six hours, I can be moderately functional. For one day at least, but several days in a row with fewer hours of rest than normal, and I'm not as friendly as I normally would be. I'm convinced to this day my inability to deal with sleep deprivation is the reason our kids started sleeping through the night within six weeks of being born. Even as babies they could see Mommy wasn't as much fun without sleep. In fact, she didn't really resemble Mommy at all. Maybe G.G. made her first hormone-fueled appearance when my children were still babies and I was too sleep-deprived to care, and in that instance, it didn't last for years and years (feels like decades), thank God.

Merriam-Webster lists "wakefulness" as a synonym for insomnia. To me, "wakefulness" implies energy, awareness, consciousness. I don't feel any of those things during my bouts of insomnia. It's more like inzombia. I'll have to sit down one of these days and compose a thoughtful letter to Merriam-Webster requesting they include it as a new word in the dictionary. It so perfectly describes how it feels; sleepless, mindless, restless, maddening, searching aimlessly, hungry. Inzombia.

It's worse on nights—or is it mornings?—like this when I was lulled into believing I would have a good night's sleep. I was tired, sleepy-tired. I was snuggled in, all cozy on my side of the bed—I still don't stray onto the other side of the bed but keep strictly to my side, except for my hand on his pillow. I fell asleep quickly.

Predictably, at around three a.m. my internal furnace switched on. I awoke struggling to throw off every stitch of blanket and sheet near my body as if they were trying to kill me. There was the requisite sweat running down my back and dotting my forehead and, as to be expected, appearing on my upper lip.

And I was angry. It's true, I wake up angry. Angry because I'm sweating. Angry because the sheets were trying to strangle me. Angry because my body feels like it's on fire. Angry because my body has betrayed me, yet again. Angry because I'm wide fucking awake at three in the morning. It's awful to wake up filled with anger, and worse to wake up feeling that way alone and not be able to fall asleep again. That's when you realize how alone you truly are.

I vary wildly about whether Nate and I would have survived this process together. Some days I flatter myself and say I'm handling it so beautifully I should lead a workshop on the process. Some days I want to set the clothes of every man I see on fire and say, "See how you like it!" I imagine Nate and I would have found our way through it together with humor. That's how we found our way through most challenges in our relationship, which with the benefit of 20/20 hindsight I can see were few and far between.

Humor was how we approached parenting. It was certainly a valuable tool to use during the tween and teen years. It saved us a lot of drama, fights, and discord. A well-timed sarcastic remark can help defuse a tense situation. It can also come back to bite you on the ass since you armed hormonal, emotionally unpredictable teenagers with sarcasm.

One of the most effective uses of humor we found was the drama flag. I had reached a breaking point with the level of emotional turmoil around friendships, boyfriends, coaches, and teachers and recall standing there watching them bicker with each other, waiting for the inevitable "Mohhhhm!" I don't know where the spark for the idea came from, I only remember wishing I had something to throw at them (something harmless, of course) to interrupt their squabble. Out of nowhere, I was picturing the penalty flag they use in football.

The same week, I cut a square out of a piece of bright yellow cloth, wrapped a rubber band several times around one corner for weight, and the drama flag was born. We kept it in the living room, and anyone could throw it when the drama was getting out of hand. It wasn't to shame anyone, but simply to interrupt the escalation of emotion.

Despite the fact it was not always appreciated, it proved to be a useful parenting tool. It gave everyone a chance to catch their breath and allowed us to laugh at ourselves for the small stuff and learn to focus on what the underlying issue was. It gave us a pause. However, like in football, there's a risk when there's a penalty flag. It may move you forward, but it can just as easily send you backward. Either way, it gives you time to regroup.

Now, at three in the morning with no husband, one daughter in college and the other on her own, I was having some trouble finding the humor, but absolutely no trouble finding the drama. As wide awake as I was, I knew sleep wasn't an option. I fleetingly entertained the idea of getting some work done, which was one of the only benefits of insomnia: I could be unexpectedly efficient at proofreading in the wee hours of the morning, like it was my superpower. But this wasn't one of those nights. I was restless, unsettled.

It was one of those moments when you feel like something bad happened and you want to call your children to make sure they're OK. They wouldn't be OK if I called them at this hour, though—they would worry something was wrong with me or their grandparents. We'd been down the road of unexpected, life-changing phone calls previously, so I would never do that to them unnecessarily.

Instead, I decided to read. Reading for pleasure isn't always fun for me, since as a proofreader and editor I already spend most of my days reading. Occasionally, though, I'm able to find a book I can lose myself in so completely that it doesn't remind me of work. God knows, the Harry Potter books helped the girls and me get through the months following Nate's death. Unfortunately, no amount of magic could make the grief disappear. I had to deal with one day at a time, with tears, rage, therapy, and girlfriends.

Tonight, I wasn't in the mood for Harry Potter. One disadvantage of relying on it after Nate's accident was there were some tricky memories associated with it no obliviate spell could erase. So, I chose a Dan Brown novel. His books have a way of engaging my curiosity and distracting me from whatever might be bothering me, plus having been raised Catholic (if going to Mass solely on major holidays counts) there is a rebellious element to it that appeals to me, like I'm breaking some rule by reading them.

I curled up on the couch with *Origin* and a cup of decaffeinated tea, determined to give myself over to the story.

The next thing I knew I was burning up and drenched in sweat again, slumped over on the couch. In the state between dreaming and waking, I felt something calling me, a nudge to wake up right now. The sky I could see through my windows was a little lighter than the last time I'd looked. I must have been asleep for a while.

I picked up my cold tea and my book, deciding to cool off on my front stoop facing the shared courtyard as I finished the chapter I'd been reading. Our neighborhood has a low instance of crime, and all of us who share the courtyard know each other fairly well. So, I wasn't concerned with being outside before dawn, though I threw my cell phone in my pocket anyway. I'm not a complete idiot.

The cool tea and the cool air on my sweaty body were exactly what I needed. They helped me ignore the nagging sensation I continued to have. It was a feeling that didn't come with instructions or any concrete information, so what good was it? But there was a feeling about it, now becoming familiar, that told me to pay attention even if it wasn't logical: a tingle starting at my neck and running down my spine.

Ignoring the feeling, I refocused on *Origin*, but it was my second time reading it, so I admit I wasn't as absorbed as I might have been. I was distracted by the sound of a mockingbird greeting the approaching day. Commuters and joggers were beginning to be out and about. Our sleepy town was awakening.

I had almost reached a state of peacefulness when my cell phone startled me by ringing in my pocket. I spilled half my tea all over myself trying to get to my phone out of my pocket and shocked a man jogging by when I let out a string of obscenities.

Trying to wipe myself off, hold my cup, my book, and my cell at the same time, and get myself inside, I called a lame apology to him. He gave me an odd glance from under his hoodie and went on his way. I noticed a strange rhythm to his footfalls as he ran, but I didn't take time to ponder it because of the terror the ringing of my phone had caused, particularly based on the thoughts I'd had earlier regarding unexpected calls.

I was relieved to see it wasn't Izzy or Bailey but was worried when I saw Jane's name. She was an early riser, but not this early.

"Jane? What's wrong?" I carried everything awkwardly to the kitchen for paper towels.

"Thank goodness you're awake. I'm all right, but the store might not be. The security company called; an alarm was triggered a short while ago. They were able to silence the alarm, but the police are there, and a window is open in the alley. It looks like someone broke in."

"Oh no. Are you there already?"

"No. I'm leaving now, but it will still take me fifteen or twenty minutes to get there."

"You want me to go and meet you there?"

"Would you?"

"No problem. I'll be there in five. What do you want me to do?"

"Oh, Liv," her voice cracked. Past Present was her baby. She loved it with all her heart. "Thank you so much. If you could be there to talk to the police, find out what you can, and keep an eye on things until I get there, I would be so grateful. You still have the key I gave you, right?"

"Of course."

While I listened, my mind raced trying to remember where I'd put the key she'd given me in case of emergency since I lived so close to the store. The key I never anticipated I'd actually need and so hadn't mentally logged where I'd put it.

"Can you please let the police in when you get there?"

"Absolutely. And I'll bring G.G. along in case they try to give me a hard time."

She laughed, which was the intended effect.

"I'll text you as soon as I get there," I said.

She disconnected and I ran to get dressed. On my way out I dug through the drawer in the table by the door until I found the key. I threw my phone into my purse and was out the door.

CHAPTER ELEVEN

I arrived at a brisk walk, not wanting to startle any police officers by running toward them and found four police cars out front. I had also seen at least two in the alley behind the store when I'd passed it on Hanover Street. I was convinced they would constitute the totality of all the police on duty in Fredericksburg on any given morning. Lights were flashing and reflecting off windows all around me. It was dizzying.

I texted Jane as I reached the store, "*Every cop car in the city is here.*"

I approached an officer standing on the sidewalk. I had come up with a plan on my way over. "Excuse me, officer."

He turned with a pasted on half-smile; no doubt ready to ask me to move along.

I had a suspicion this would be the tactic, which is why I had a plan. I drew on my inner G.G., consciously for a change, held out my hand, and tried to exude an air of authority with a touch of bitchiness.

"I'm Olivia Wilde. I'm a partner in Past Present. The primary owner, Jane Harper, is on her way. She told me there has been a break-in. Is that true?" I spoke all of this in a rapid-fire, worried but confident tone, hoping he would take me at my word. I clinched the deal with, "Do you need me to unlock the door?"

I reached into my bag for the key, which I had placed on my key ring.

That did it. "Yes, ma'am. That would be extremely helpful. Two of our officers are in the alley at the point of entry, which appears to have been the bathroom window. We were going to cut through the lock on the front door so we can sweep the premises for intruders. We've seen no movement inside, but we need to verify the building is secure."

I stepped forward with the key outstretched, knowing how upset Jane would be if they had cut through the lock.

Officer Clark, by his name badge, put his hand on my arm. "Ma'am. I can't let you touch the door before it's dusted for fingerprints. May I have the key, please?"

I removed the store key from the ring and handed it to him.

"Please wait across the street until we've secured the premises," he said.

Another officer who had been waiting next to one of the police cars radioed they were going inside and joined him in front of the store.

I thanked them and quickly crossed the street. I started pacing up and down the sidewalk, trying to ignore the stares of people who were passing by with more frequency, all most likely on their way to their coffee shop of choice, of which there were several. A couple people stopped alongside me and together we watched as Officer Clark and the other officer entered the store with their hands on their holstered weapons.

My phone kept vibrating in my hand, and when I stopped watching the store long enough to look at it, I found there were three texts from Jane, all filling me in on her progress from her home in Stafford County not far from the county courthouse. She was obviously using voice to text while driving, based on the mixed-up words. If she was truly passing seventh heaven rather than a 7-11, then I wanted a map for her route into town.

I decided calling her would be easier than texting. I didn't even get a word out before her voice came tumbling out of the phone.

"What's going on? Is there any damage? Was anything stolen? Have they caught anyone?"

It was only because she had no choice but to pause for breath that I was able to speak. "Slow down. I just let them in the front door so they wouldn't have to cut the lock."

"Oh, Lord."

"They're inside now making sure there's no one still inside the store. There are at least six police cars here. So don't be shocked when you arrive."

"Did you get the name of the officer in charge? I'll be there in a second, and I'll need to talk to whoever is in charge. Have they let you inside? Is there damage?"

"Jane, try to breathe. I don't know if there's any damage inside yet, but I don't see any on the outside. I had to tell them I'm—"

The phone went dead. As I pivoted for the next lap of my pacing route, I saw her swerve around the corner onto Caroline Street. She skidded to a halt in her Honda Pilot in the parking spot in front of me, startling the new officer who'd arrived to guard the door.

She jumped out of her car and gave me a quick side hug and took a step toward the street.

I grabbed her arm and explained we had to wait for them to verify no one was inside and it was safe to enter.

Her eyes widened at the thought someone might still be in her store.

"How the hell did you get here so fast? You must've been flying."

This at least brought a little smile. "Well, you said every cop in the city was here, so I figured I could get away with speeding."

We fell into pacing together, but it wasn't long until we saw Officer Clark come to the door and wave me over.

It was all Jane needed; she went straight to work.

I realized I hadn't finished warning her I told them I was a partner in the business so they wouldn't send me away, but she moved so fast I didn't get a chance. I trailed behind, in her wake of authority.

She wasted no time getting inside the building and went straight to the person she determined was the officer in charge, who was standing with Officer Clark. The female officer on the sidewalk held the door for me and I stepped inside.

Jane had already opened her office door and led the two officers inside. I couldn't make out what they were saying but saw she went to the closet and bent down, reaching for an object on the floor. Moving a step closer I could see it was a safe. She opened it, pulled out a tray, and rifled through it. She replaced the tray, reset the lock, and turned to Officer Clark.

He handed her the key I'd given him and said something while gesturing over his shoulder at me. I saw Jane's eyebrows rise a tiny bit. She stole a glance at me, a hint of a smile on her lips, and glossed right over whatever he'd said, giving nothing away.

She peppered them with several questions and showed them to the door of the rare books room. Finally, I could hear their conversation.

"Besides some of the more valuable jewelry, which is kept in locked cases across from my office, this is where I keep the most valuable items I sell. That's why it has its own security code. I didn't get an alert the alarm on this room was tripped. After we check in here, I'll call the security company and have them review the system for any logins, but no one else has the code but me."

"Not even your partner?" asked the senior officer, nodding his head in my direction.

"No. She's more of a silent partner."

It was the first time anyone's called me a silent anything.

She punched in the code, and they entered the room and closed the door behind them, cutting me off from their conversation. I watched the three of them walk around the room briefly and then Jane exited, leaving them there looking around skeptically. She signaled for me to follow her into her office.

By the time I sat down across from her, she was already navigating the security company's menu options on the phone.

She looked through the window between the two rooms, and seeing they weren't watching us, mouthed, "Partner?"

I shrugged sheepishly and whispered, "I was afraid they would've sent me away otherwise."

She held up her hand to stop me as someone came on the line.

"This is Jane Harper at seven seventeen Caroline Street in Fredericksburg, customer number 12672. I spoke to you earlier about shutting off the alarm at my store for the police. I fear this will be pointless, but I need to see if there were any logins on my secondary security system after eight p.m. last night."

She barely let them respond before she interrupted, "Yes, I know the main system was triggered this morning on a rear window." She rolled her eyes at their obvious stupidity.

"You should be able to see I have a secondary system in the building for a specific room. It should be listed as Rare Books."

More murmuring emanated from the phone. Jane's perfectly manicured fingernails drummed on the desk.

"What?" The drumming stopped abruptly. "But that's impossible. What time?"

A pause again while she listened and wrote on a notepad. "It just can't be. You're certain?"

Now the murmuring sounded impatient.

"Can you send the log to me by email? Yes, as soon as possible. I will need to show it to the police while they're here. Thank you."

She hung up before they could possibly have responded. She was pale and her jaw hung open slightly.

"Someone entered the code after you left?"

"At three thirty-four a.m." She started to say more but was interrupted by a knock at the door. Officer Clark and the other officer, whose last name I discovered was Howard, stepped inside the small office. Officer Howard sat down in a ladder-back chair at the side of the desk while Clark remained standing.

"I take it you're surprised by the news from the security company," Officer Howard said.

I had to make a concerted effort to keep G.G. from saying, "No shit, Sherlock."

Officer Obvious continued, "What did they say?"

Jane composed herself before speaking. "They said the code for the door on the rare books room was entered at three thirty-four this morning."

"And you're positive no one else had the code for that door?" Did he shoot a sideways glance at me when he asked that?

"No. No one."

"None of your employees? Or are there other partners?"

"No. I will give the code to an employee, usually my assistant manager, if I'm going out of town for a book show or going on vacation, which I hardly ever do, but I always change it when I get back."

She rushed on when seeing his reaction. "I trust all my employees. I'm just super paranoid about things like that. I change my passwords all the time. Ask Liv."

"She's completely nuts about that kind of thing. She won't even tell any of her friends her password for her phone. I swear they all know mine. We're always trying to trick her into giving it to us so we can post bogus things on her social media accounts." Jane's scowl told me not only was I not helping, but I was also possibly making things worse, so I stopped short.

Jane took control of the conversation before what I'd said about trying to steal her passwords could register with the officers. "What I don't understand is the timing. Whoever it was accessed the book room at three thirty-four, but the alarm on the window wasn't tripped until four thirty-five. How come there was no alarm triggered when they entered the building? How did they get in without setting it off, but set it off going out?"

I barely had time to glimpse the puzzlement in Jane's and Officer Howard's expressions before another voice spoke from behind us.

A woman as tall as Clark, but older than him and Howard, stepped out from behind where Clark stood. "There's only one answer to that question that makes any sense. The suspect or suspects were inside the building when you left."

Jane's jaw dropped as she absorbed the statement.

The woman wore black pants, a navy polo shirt with a Fredericksburg Police Department patch on the chest, and a lightweight black FPD jacket. She wore a lanyard around her neck holding her badge.

She crossed the room with her hand outstretched to Jane. "Good morning, ma'am. I'm Detective Gomez. I'll be coordinating the investigation of this case." She nodded a greeting at the other two officers.

Howard made to stand up to surrender his chair to her, but she put her hand out to stop him.

"I'm fine here. Thank you." She pulled out a notebook and pen from her pants pocket, then addressed me. "How are you involved with this situation?"

I was distracted by the gun I now saw in a holster on her hip, so Jane spoke up for me. "She's a silent partner in the business. I called her as soon as I was notified by the security company and asked her to come down here. She lives a few blocks away, so I knew she could get here before me."

I nodded my assent to all of the above.

"She can remain for the questioning if you would like." Jane nodded and Detective Gomez got right down to business. "You haven't discovered anything missing yet, correct?"

Sounding exasperated, Jane said, "I haven't had time to go through everything yet. I'm anxious to get back in the rare book room to see if anything is missing, since whoever it was apparently had access to that room." Jane's brow creased as she watched two other officers moving around the room wearing gloves, searching for evidence the thief might have left behind.

"The most important question is how soon can we get access to your security camera footage?" Gomez paused for a beat and continued, "Are you aware the cameras have been tampered with?"

Surprise showed in Jane's expression. "What?"

Apparently satisfied this was news to Jane, she said, "There is black spray paint on the lenses."

Jane grabbed her laptop and after a few clicks had opened the program linked to the security cameras. She rotated the computer so Detective Gomez could see it. The boxes on the screen, which should be showing parts of the store, now showed only black. Tears welled in her eyes.

"Do you record the footage on this computer or is it done remotely by the security company?" Gomez asked.

Jane dropped her gaze to her desk, took a breath, and said, "I don't record it."

"You have the cameras installed, but don't record anything?" Gomez asked.

"That's unfortunately correct. I had the cameras installed mainly to monitor things while the store is open to prevent shoplifting. There are signs around warning the cameras are in use, hoping it will prevent people from stealing."

"Seems like an awful lot of trouble to go to if you're not going to record anything."

Jane's jaw tensed. "I had them installed by the security company intending to have them used for recording, but after they were in place, I found out I had not been made aware of all the ongoing fees required for that feature. In the end, I had to settle for using them to deter shoplifting, which is a bigger problem than you might imagine at the antique stores around here. I wanted to replace them with a system I could record and monitor myself, but I decided it wasn't worth the expense since we've never had trouble beyond the shoplifting." She ran her fingers through her short, brown hair, which while normally perfectly coiffed, was this morning unintentionally pointing in several directions at once.

Detective Gomez gave her a sympathetic look. "I'm assuming you don't keep large sums of cash in the register?"

"No. We balance it each night. I take the day's deposit with me and lock the small amount we keep on hand in the cash drawer in a safe in the closet." She gestured to the closet behind her. "I went through it with Officer Clark and the cash is all there."

Clark nodded in agreement, so Gomez went on.

"I understand you're worried about the rest of the store. Why don't you take a quick walk around. Look for anything that's out of place, not only for missing items, but please don't touch anything. I will find out how soon you'll be able to get into the book room. If you notice anything out of the ordinary, let one of us know."

She left the office, followed by Clark and Howard. They stood together outside the book room door. Gomez spoke to them and pointed around the store before stepping into the book room. The other two began wandering around the store.

Jane's body language told me how tired she was.

I leaned across the desk and squeezed one of her hands. "Are you OK?"

"I don't understand it. How could someone have been hiding in the store when I left?"

All I could do was shrug. The thought was unsettling for both of us.

"Doesn't someone help you close up?" I asked.

"Yes. But there are a fair number of times when I stay to finish some paperwork or process online orders I didn't get to during the day." Shock registered on her face. "What if I had stayed later? What would have happened if—?" She couldn't even finish the sentence.

"No what ifs," I said. I got up and went behind the desk and bent down to hug her. She was trembling. "Let's go walk around the store. Maybe they didn't find anything valuable enough for them and gave up."

Her eyebrows were raised doubtfully, but we headed out into the store anyway.

As we began wandering through the aisles, I put my arm around her shoulders. Jane is an incredibly independent person, who rarely needs propping up, so I knew how shook up she was when she didn't shrug my arm off, but instead grasped my hand where it rested on her shoulder.

We continued wandering around, careful not to touch anything. The movement helped calm her down.

Her ring tone went off, disrupting our wandering and any calm she'd felt. She saw the number and was all professionalism again as she accepted the call. She stopped and listened. The voice coming from the phone was high pitched and frantic.

"Calm down, Ellie." Her eyes rolled heavenward, as if pleading for patience and strength. "I don't suppose it should come as a shock to me you heard about it already. Everything is all right. I haven't found any damage to the store. However, there's not much chance we'll be opening today. Give me time to finish sorting things out with the police and I will let you know if I can still use your help today."

The pitch of Ellie's voice had not come down at all as it came spilling out of the phone in another torrent of questions.

"Eleanor. Please calm down. I'm fine. The store is fine. I can't talk anymore right now. I will call you as soon as I can."

Ellie apparently needed more reassurance, so I left Jane to try to calm her down as I strolled into the next aisle.

I thought about what Detective Gomez had suggested: *Look for anything that's out of place, not only for missing items.* I figured it would be easy. Looking for things that are out of place is what I do all day while proofing and editing. I roamed to the next aisle with no luck.

As I approached the end of the aisle, I turned around and still didn't see anything, but I definitely felt something. The heat started to kick in. I paused as the hot coals residing in the center of my back were stoked by whatever mysterious force controlled them. The sweat beaded on my forehead and upper lip and began to drip down over my shoulder blades.

I groped in my pocket for the hair-tie I always carry for un-expected, yet expected, heat waves. As I drew it out, my ring caught on the edge of my pocket and caused me to drop the hair-tie. I was inclined to leave it there on the floor under the old child's school desk where it had fallen. I could just stand there and fan myself rather than put the now-dusty thing in my hair. Yet the prickly sensation started once more, so I heeded the quiet voice in my mind that said, "Pick it up."

I reached under the desk.

Again, the voice came loud and clear, this time repeating Gomez's words, "Out of place."

My hand on the hair-tie, I replied, "Fuck off," and abruptly stood up, knocking my head on the edge of the desk, which, of course, made me drop the damn thing a second time.

Rubbing my head, I leaned back down. This time as I bent over, I saw an object under a dresser farther down the aisle. Standing up, I pulled my hair up into a kind of messy ball (it wasn't quite long enough for a full ponytail) and retraced my steps down the row.

I squatted down in front of the dresser. Its base curved in from the corners and formed a delicate point in the middle. It was behind the point that I glimpsed a shiny wrapper, it appeared to be the kind a granola bar would come in.

It may not have jumped out as being out of place to some-one who didn't know Jane, but I know how militant she is about people not bringing food and drinks into the store. On weekends, she always has an employee stationed near the front door to prevent any violations of the policy. I've seen Jane stop moms at the door who are pushing a stroller with a tray full of Cheerios, sticky fingerprints, and a sippy cup. The employees are allowed to have food in the tiny kitchen, but nowhere else. They aren't allowed any drinks while working in the front of the store, not even coffee. It had been the deal breaker for many a millennial employee.

So how did a granola bar, which by the state of the dirty wrapper was coated in chocolate, escape their notice?

I looked more closely around the aisle I was in. Jane was still trying to end her conversation with Ellie a couple rows over now and smiled to myself as I rotated slowly in a circle. It was an aisle featuring mainly bedroom furniture. There were several dressers, which I guessed were from different decades of the 20th century. One had an ornate mirror attached to it. If it hadn't been for the mirror, I might have missed it, as I had when walking in the other direction. Since I was supposed to take note of anything out of place, though, the slender gap in the doors on the armoire across the aisle, which I saw reflected in the mirror, had caught my attention.

"Find anything?" Detective Gomez asked, making me jump out of my skin. I hadn't heard her coming. "I didn't mean to startle you."

"No, I kinda zoned out." I fanned myself with my hand. "It happens sometimes."

"Ah. Roger that. I completely understand."

And I thought perhaps she did. She was old enough to understand. There was some gray in her short, wavy brown hair and a few lines at the corners of her eyes. I decided I kinda liked her.

I wondered what she'd had to go through to become a detective in a small city in Virginia as a woman, let alone a woman of color. I had begun to understand on a different level the discrimination people of color encounter through conversations with Claire and Jonathan about what he's dealt with throughout his life as an African American. It's enough to drive me batshit crazy, thinking of him having to live with the everyday microaggressions and flat-out racism. The stories Claire has shared about the crap their daughters have had to put up with from some of the students in the county schools because their skin tones more closely resemble their father's was infuriating and deeply sad.

So, it could have been my love for Claire and her family that softened me a little toward Gomez. I don't have a poor relationship with the police, there's simply a part of my brain that automatically associates them with Nate's death.

I decided to trust her and pointed at the dresser.

She looked at the dresser and then at me with a single raised eyebrow. "Yes?"

"There's a wrapper, from a granola bar under the dresser right there." I pointed to the floor.

"And?"

Now it was my turn for raised eyebrows—plural, I can't raise only one. I drew out and emphasized my first word: "And, it feels strange."

I watched her body language change slightly at the word "feels," but I pushed on.

"It *is* strange. Jane is militant about not allowing any food or drinks in the store. Besides, you said to notice anything out of place, right?"

She nodded.

"A dirty wrapper is definitely out of place and it's under the dresser directly across from the armoire, whose door is open a crack." I realized I said the last part sort of triumphantly, as if I had discovered a lost tomb of the pharaohs. I tried to hold Gomez's gaze with what I hoped was dignity.

After a beat and what might have been a grin she was trying to resist, she knelt down and retrieved the wrapper from under the dresser, holding it carefully in a gloved hand. Next, she inspected the front of the armoire. "It wouldn't be too unusual for the door to be open. I would guess the hinges on these old pieces have seen better days."

Jane's voice from over her shoulder preempted whatever she might have said next. "Where on earth did that come from? There's chocolate all over it. Detective Gomez, I really must insist you not eat or drink anything at all in the store."

We were still looking at each other and Gomez's lips were fighting a grin again, but she faced Jane, and I didn't get to see if the grin won.

When she spoke, she was all business, no hint of humor in her tone. "Your partner here found it under a dresser. I'd say it's not very old. The chocolate is still soft and there are no bugs on it." She walked to the end of the aisle, calling for Officer Clark to bring an evidence bag.

We followed her and he quickly approached with a bag in hand. Gomez was still holding the wrapper delicately from one corner as she placed it in the bag, making a notation on the outside of it before handing it to Clark.

Gomez glanced past me down the aisle. I stepped to the side so I wouldn't block her view. Jane opened her mouth to speak, but I held up my hand to stop her as Gomez stepped past me. She didn't continue down the aisle, but instead squatted down where she was.

Just when I thought she was going to stand, she settled her knees on the floor, put her hands down in front of her and lowered her head to the ground, tilting it sideways so her right cheek was almost touching the floor. She remained there momentarily, looking down the aisle. Jane and I watched her without making a sound. She pulled her phone from her pocket and took a couple photos of the floor from her prone position.

Finally, she stood, brushed off her knees, and addressed Jane. "How often are the floors cleaned?"

"The cleaning crew comes on Monday, Wednesday, and Friday evenings as soon as we close. There's always someone here while they're here, usually it's me wrapping up the receipts for the day. If the floors are messy on other days, we sweep them ourselves after we close."

Tracking Gomez's train of thought, I knew it meant the cleaning crew was not here last night because it was Sunday.

"Did you have to sweep up last night?" Gomez asked.

"No. It was a relatively slow day. Not much traffic all weekend, unfortunately. So, I didn't bother," Jane replied. "Why?"

Gomez signaled to Clark. "Excuse me, ladies. Please don't go down the remainder of this aisle for now." She pressed a button on her phone and waited for an answer as she walked away.

We both spun around and automatically squatted down. The cleaning crew does a fairly good job, but we could see they don't get all the way under all the furniture lining the aisles. There were dust bunnies under the center of almost everything, beyond where their cleaning devices could reach.

"I can see I need to talk to the cleaning staff, but I don't see anything else of importance," Jane said. "I'm going to go find out when I can open the store."

She stood and strode off in the direction of her office where Gomez was talking on her phone and with Clark simultaneously.

I settled on my knees and lowered my cheek to the linoleum as Detective Gomez had, to get my eye closer to the floor. I repeated her actions, rotating my head first one way and then the other.

I had to take a couple glances back and forth and under the desk next to me to the adjacent aisle to see any difference.

It was slight, but her practiced eye had seen it with one look. There was an area on the floor in front of the armoire that was slightly different from the other portions of the aisle. I saw it only when compared to the edges of the aisle, where I could see the remnants of a weekend of doors opening and furniture decaying. Even with little traffic in the store over the weekend, or possibly because there wasn't a lot of traffic over the weekend, I could see a thin layer of dirt and dust on the floor extending from where I was kneeling until right before the armoire. It didn't start again until the opposite end of the armoire.

It was as if right in front of the armoire something or someone had removed whatever dirt might have accumulated there, but I had no idea how it was significant.

I stood up and saw Detective Gomez watching me, one eyebrow raised.

CHAPTER TWELVE

O n rare occasions we have called an emergency Monthly.
Though I'm positive this was our first on a Monday
night, as it usually takes a few more workdays before anyone
finds they need it. By one o'clock the afternoon of the break-in,
Jane had shared the news with all of us by text. Truth be told,
we'd all known by then. Despite what my daughters might say,
the old-fashioned grapevine can move faster than texts in a small
community like ours.

After everyone had written their obligatory consolation texts,
Jane sent out what we referred to as the Bat-Signal, for an
emergency gathering. It was our code. It wasn't written down
anywhere, but you were pretty much required to set everything
else aside and show up when anyone invoked the Bat-Signal.
Anyone could convene an emergency Monthly when in need,
but since it meant everyone had to change their plans on short
notice, we used it sparingly.

At least, in a normal year we used it sparingly. Following
Nate's accident, it got used repeatedly over six or seven months,
but that was an extreme circumstance. I sent up the signal only

once during that period. The other times were when my friends were particularly worried about me. It's a gift to have friends who can see and sense your signals even when you can't bring yourself to send them.

Jane's text followed the simple code we had developed over time—the flashlight emoji followed by the bat emoji, for the Bat-Signal, followed by emojis reflecting the nature of the emotional need. In this case it was angry swearing emoji, crying emoji, angry swearing emoji. Then she gave the place and time: 7:30 Red Dragon. For emergency gatherings, it had become customary for us to meet at a restaurant or bar rather than someone's home so no last-minute cleaning would be required. This custom was, of course, contingent upon there not being a lot of crying required either. If that was the case, a more private venue was called for.

Meeting at the Red Dragon Brewery gave me a clue about Jane's state of mind. She wanted a place where we could talk without everyone in the bar trying to eavesdrop. When it's busy, there's enough ambient noise at the brewery, along with cement floors and nothing to dampen their echoey nature, to allow you to have a semi-private conversation while still meeting in town. When we absolutely didn't want everyone we knew to be privy to what we were talking about, like when Hannah needed to discuss her affair, we met at a bar out at the mall. There's a wider mix of people there and loud music always playing. Additionally, the location she chose told me Jane needed a beer.

While they serve a limited number of cocktails and some bar food, the Red Dragon is known for their range of craft beers.

Perhaps not surprisingly, Jane was the last to arrive. She sat down with an exaggerated sigh when she finally arrived closer to 7:45 than the appointed meeting time. We all had cold glasses of beer in front of us already, mine was the Road Rash Red Ale.

"I'm sorry I'm late. It felt like the police were there forever this morning and there were a million phone calls, most of them from people wanting all the details. It threw off my whole day. Then Ellie and I had to get the place cleaned up so we can open in the morning. Lord knows we'll be busy tomorrow. I should require a purchase in exchange for information." She craned her neck around, to read the beer list hanging above the bar.

I signaled our server. I had warned her when our last friend arrived, she was going to need a beer as quickly as possible. She had taken me at my word and came right over.

She wasn't even able to get a word out before Jane said, "I'll take an Off Your Trolley, please. It perfectly reflects how I'm feeling."

Jane didn't give the server another thought, but I smiled at her and mouthed, "Thank you."

She smiled and went straight to the bar for the beer. She was placing the drink in front of Jane before we'd done more than say hello and ask how she was doing.

Jane finally acknowledged our server, whose name tag said "Peggy."

"Bless you for getting that so quickly."

Peggy smiled and moved on to another table.

Jane took a deep draft of the beer, closed her eyes, and took another. We let her settle in and catch her breath before peppering her with questions.

The reprieve didn't last long.

Mary jumped in first. "Tell us what happened. There are all kinds of rumors swirling around."

Jane sighed. "That didn't take long, did it? It's been what, sixteen hours since I got the call? What kind of rumors are there?"

Mary wasn't a gossip, but she was the Fredericksburg native in the group, which meant she was connected to all the various outlets for news via the grapevine. Most of the time, it proved to be handy. It's how we found out Hannah's husband Simon was having an affair.

"It's mostly exaggeration, as far as I can tell. The most wildly off-base version I heard was when you arrived to open the store you came upon a naked burglar, who shoved you down and rode off on a bike."

"Ouch," said Jane. "Naked bike riding sounds painful."

"Where do people get this stuff?" asked Claire. "Do they just make it up entirely? Or is it like a game of telephone, and it gets muddled the more it gets passed?"

"I'd say it gets muddled the more people get pissed!" I raised my glass, and all the ladies joined me.

We put our glasses down and Jane looked up to find us all staring at her.

She rolled her eyes and began her story from the time the call woke her from her sleep. There were parts of it that had occurred after I'd left that stood out to me. Gomez and her team had dusted most of the store for fingerprints, paying particular attention to the armoire and the floor in front of it. They had also swept the dust and debris out of the wardrobe into an evidence bag, and had an officer take pictures of "everything but my ass," according to Jane.

"Don't be so sure," giggled Claire. "They may have taken pictures of that too."

"It *is* quite a nice ass," Sophie added.

Jane concurred with a smile and a pat on her backside. "They'll need all my store staff to go to the police station tomorrow so they can get their fingerprints. They say it's so they can see if there are any prints other than staff on things like the door of the rare book room or the bathroom window. But what good can it do when we have different customers every day?"

"Do they really believe there was someone in the store the whole time while you were closing things up for the night?" asked Hannah.

"Yes, they do. And I have to agree with them. I can't think of another scenario to explain it," Jane admitted.

"That's so creepy," Claire said. "Where could someone have been hiding?"

Jane gestured to me. "Detective Wilde here found a granola bar wrapper near an armoire. They suspect he might have been hiding in there."

"He?" asked Mary.

Jane replied, "He, she, it. The shit who broke into my store. I don't know, can you even call it a break-in if they were there all along? It was more of a break-out."

"I don't care what you call it. I'm just glad you didn't come across the son of a bitch while you were closing up," said Mary. I could tell she was upset, because normally she favored "son of a biscuit."

We all fell silent, trying not to visualize what might have transpired if she had come upon the intruder, but there was no doubt we were all imagining precisely that.

To stop my own frightening train of thought more than anything, I asked, "Did you find anything missing?"

"Not yet. I didn't have time to go through everything though with all their questions and interruptions and all the phone calls. They want me to do an inventory of the rare book room as soon as possible. I would be there doing it now if I felt comfortable being there alone."

"You shouldn't stay there after closing on your own anymore," Hannah admonished. "I never liked you doing that."

Jane threw up her hands. "But I can't afford to pay someone to sit there doing nothing just so I'm not alone."

I felt the internal furnace fire up, accompanied by the feeling something was about to happen. I took another sip of my beer to cool me down and to ignore the anticipation I could feel rising for no apparent reason.

The reason became clear when Sophie said, "You know, Liv is kind of a psychic detective." She smiled at me and continued, "She told me where I could find my phone a couple weeks ago and there was absolutely no way she could have known where I'd left it so specifically. She might be able to help you figure out what they stole or even who did it."

Suddenly everyone was staring at me instead of Jane. A couple of them were chuckling, thinking it was a joke.

The heat increased throughout my body and began popping up on my forehead as beads of sweat. "It was a fluke," I protested.

"You didn't think I'd forgotten, did you?" Sophie asked, a mischievous tone in her voice.

"A girl can hope." Everyone kept looking at me, not letting me off the hook. "Thanks for nothing, Soph," I muttered. "I have a new suggestion for where you can put your phone," I said while glaring at her.

Sophie didn't give up so easily. "Calm down, G.G. Don't get your panties in a bunch," she teased. "Come on. It's for Jane's sake. Any ideas?"

I suddenly found my beer glass extremely interesting. "It's not some trick I can conjure up on demand."

My body temperature continued to rise from the heat of their stares and the hot flash. I tried to concentrate on Jane and how much the store meant to her. I closed my eyes and took a deep breath to try to shut everything else out. I tried to let the sense of knowing making my whole body tingle envelop me.

Like when I saw Sophie putting her phone in her pocket, I suddenly saw the box of books in the rare book room in my mind. I opened my eyes and meeting Jane's curious gaze, the words coming out of my mouth before I could think better of it said, "You could double check the box of books."

"The one in the book room?" she asked.

I nodded.

"It was still sealed this morning when I went through the room with the police. Why that box?"

I tried to shrug it off. "It's just a feeling," I said, wondering why I had opened my big mouth and shooting Sophie another dirty look, which she simply ignored.

"You should start with that box first thing in the morning. Trust me," said Sophie.

I felt cornered with them all staring at me. "What? It will probably amount to nothing."

Jane took pity on me and changed the subject. "What I want to know is how on Earth they got the security code. That has to dramatically narrow down the number of people it can be. I changed the number after the holidays when I had extra seasonal help in the store, but I can't believe any of my employees would hide out in the store or watch me enter the code and give it to someone else."

"Did the police have any ideas about how they got it?" asked Mary.

"They're convinced it means it must be an inside job. I tried to tell them anyone who works there would know there isn't anything so valuable it would be worth going to such lengths to steal," Jane said, exasperated.

"You have a point. If it was an employee, why wouldn't they have found a way to take whatever it was when you were at lunch or on one of your days off?"

"Exactly," said Jane. She raised her hand, called, "Peggy!" and downed the rest of her beer.

We wandered out of the bar around 9:30. Sophie convinced Jane to get an Uber to drive her home, which is what we typically do after our Monthlies. She said she would be glad to have the driver drop me off on the way, but it was in the opposite direction. Besides, I only lived a few blocks from the Red Dragon and the crime rate is relatively low in the downtown area. So, I waved off the offer and headed home.

It was a beautiful night. The air had a softness to it that comes with spring and while there was a chill in the air, it was warm enough for the light sweater I had on to keep me warm.

When I made the right onto Caroline Street, I almost ran into a jogger. Thanks to his quick reflexes, he was able to dodge me, hardly missing a step. I offered my apology to his sweaty back, which was bare right down to his flimsy running shorts. My gaze lingered on his retreating form, and I lamented how long it had been since I'd caused a man to sweat.

The beer must've affected me more than I thought it had. I giggled and redirected myself to my original path toward home, with a nagging thought hidden somewhere in my partly clouded brain.

CHAPTER THIRTEEN

Two days later I was dozing at my computer, tired from another night of inzombia, when my phone chiming three times in quick succession brought me to consciousness. That meant it was either Jane or Izzy. Neither one had the patience to hit return in a text message to start a new thought. Instead, they always sent multiple texts in a row.

I was partially right. Two of them were from Jane. The other was a reminder I had set for myself, which prompted swearing. I must have done more than doze because I found I had only twenty minutes before I needed to be at the museum to meet up with Claire.

I opened the texts from Jane and swore again.

Gomez wants to see both of us for follow-up questions about the break-in. Meet me at the police station at 2.

I was not being invited but summoned, though whether it was Jane's directive or Detective Gomez's wasn't clear.

Claire and I were planning to eat in the museum's garden if things weren't busy. She was expecting me there in a half-hour and I hadn't packed any food yet, let alone got myself ready.

I sent a quick text to Jane confirming I could meet her at the police station and then ran around throwing together a salad and trying to make myself presentable to go out in public for the afternoon.

Hopefully only appearing slightly disheveled, I took my usual path to the James Monroe Museum, wandering past the library, up Lewis Street crossing Caroline Street and past the Historic Fredericksburg Foundation, across Princess Anne Street and left on to Charles within site of the Mary Washington House. Every time I made the trek, I smiled at the history to be found in so many parts of our city.

Not having spent any extended time in the southern states prior to relocating to Fredericksburg, I was shocked by how much the Civil War still reverberates here. However, after I'd been here a few years, I found the lasting effects of it are felt all the time in Virginia if you're paying attention, and some people can't avoid it even if they wanted to. It came up last week when Claire called me while driving to work.

"I just need to vent." Those were the first words out of her mouth. It was a shorthand we'd learned over years of friendship. If we needed to get something off our chest without anyone trying to fix it, we would say it right up front. She didn't even say hello first, so I knew immediately how upset she was.

"OK. I'm listening," I said.

"I really think we need to move." Claire said this fairly frequently. She lives in Spotsylvania County, west and south of Fredericksburg. "I'm so tired of seeing the Confederate flag."

Her voice expressed exactly how tired of it she was. "What the hell is the matter with people?"

"I wish I knew."

"I know the universe is supposed to bend toward justice, but one of these days I'm afraid justice is going to be me ripping a goddamn flagpole down or tearing the bumper off someone's car and shoving it—" She stopped herself. "I'm sorry. It just makes me so angry. And then I consider how Jonathan and the girls feel being stuck behind cars with ignorant, hateful bumper stickers, or how they feel when they drive by the flags."

There was nothing I could say to make it any easier, so I didn't say anything, but sat with her in silence until she'd parked her car and felt calm enough to be able to engage with visitors at the museum.

We'd been having similar conversations for years, but the problem of racism was even more painfully apparent to my friends and me in August 2017, when the loathsome Unite the Right rally was held not far away in Charlottesville. We had watched the footage on the news with Confederate flags and swastikas side-by-side and the resulting death of a young woman, a young woman who could have been any of our daughters or sons.

I felt a chill at the memory of that day and its echoes in my recent conversation with Claire, so I crossed William Street, moving out of the shade of the buildings, grateful for the warmth of the sun. It had finally emerged from the gray clouds that had brought rain earlier in the week, and its warmth was beginning to chase the chill of the memories away. I strolled the last half block to the museum soaking up the sun's warmth and focusing on the lovely weather we were going to have for lunch in the garden.

I passed through the wrought-iron gate marking the entrance to the museum, walked under the crepe myrtle tree that graces the garden, and proceeded to the bright red entry door. The chime rang as I entered, and I waved to Claire, who was in the room to my left orienting a family of four to the museum.

She was in the midst of her introduction but waved hello without missing a beat.

"The museum sits on property that belonged to James Monroe when he first moved his young wife, Elizabeth Kortright Monroe, to his home state of Virginia and began a law practice in Fredericksburg. The brick buildings housing the collection were not on the property in 1786 when Monroe purchased it. They were built after Monroe owned the property and were joined together over the years. They were set to be demolished in 1927, when descendants of James Monroe intervened and saved the site, subsequently creating the museum with artifacts the family had handed down through the generations. Monroe's great, great grandson, Laurence Gouverneur Hoes, presided over the museum as its director for fifty years. The museum still hosts reunions for the Monroes' descendants every five years or so."

The parents were interested, and their teenaged sons were decidedly disinterested.

Claire carried on, but I saw her peek at the boys. "By all accounts, Elizabeth Kortright Monroe was a beauty and their relationship affectionate. They were married in February 1786 and made the move to Fredericksburg that fall when Elizabeth was seven months pregnant. Their first daughter, Eliza, was born here in December of the same year."

I liked to imagine Elizabeth Monroe and I had something in common. She was born and raised in New York, so moving from the north to a southern town like Fredericksburg was an adjustment for her, as moving from Jersey to Fredericksburg was for me. When I first learned about her, I found myself hoping she was able to make some good friends while she was here, too. It must have been overwhelming to be a new wife, a new mother, and moving to a new state simultaneously. There was a vast difference between New York City and Fredericksburg in 1786, as there still is today.

Elizabeth and I also had an affectionate relationship with our husbands in common.

"Family was important to them, so Monroe's wife and daughters accompanied him when he was appointed Minister to France by George Washington in 1794," Claire continued. "To the French she was known as la belle américaine."

I've been to France too, but for whatever reason that's not what they called me.

Claire began listing the many public service positions Monroe had held, but saw that while the parents appeared impressed, the two boys were finding their phones more interesting.

I leaned against the doorframe and watched Claire work her magic.

She asked the boys how old they were. When they shared they were sixteen and seventeen, she asked, "Can you picture yourselves being in college already or going off to fight in the American Revolution to overthrow the government only a year or two older than you are now?"

They still weren't overly engaged, but they did glance up at Claire.

"James Monroe entered the College of William and Mary at the age of sixteen and by the age of seventeen had taken part in a raid on the Powder Horn and the Governor's Palace to steal weapons and ammunition for the revolution. At the age of eighteen, he became a lieutenant in the Continental Army's Third Virginia Infantry Regiment and went on to serve under General George Washington in several important battles and was quartered with the Continental Army's forces at Valley Forge."

She then pointed to an iconic image of Washington crossing the Delaware. "Have you seen this painting in any of your history studies?"

The boys nodded.

She lowered her voice when she spoke again. "It's a lie."

Their expressions were skeptical.

"Do you see the man behind Washington holding the American flag?"

They looked at the painting, nodded. Their parents were smiling at Claire.

"It's meant to be James Monroe. However, he wasn't with Washington when he crossed the Delaware. Monroe crossed the Delaware River ahead of the main body of troops with a cousin of General Washington as part of an advance guard. Their mission was to guard an important crossroads near Trenton and prevent anyone from passing so they wouldn't be able to bring word of the Continental army's approach to the British and Hessian troops. Monroe and his fellow soldiers stood their ground all night through snow, sleet, rain, and hail. Anyone who tried to pass was held captive in the nearby woods. The events of that night proved to be lifesaving for James Monroe."

The boys were finally listening attentively.

"The soldiers' presence was noticed by the dogs in a nearby house. The owner of the house was alerted by their barking, and seeing the troops in the road, he went storming out into the snow to confront them. Once the man discovered they were American soldiers rather than British, he offered them food, which they gratefully accepted, while refusing to leave their posts to eat in the man's warm home.

"The man was Dr. John Riker. Dr. Riker resolved to go with the army into Trenton the next day. During the Battle of Trenton, James Monroe was struck in the left shoulder by a musket ball, which he carried in his shoulder the rest of his life. He would most likely have bled to death from the wound if the doctor had not been at the battle to tend to his injury."

I removed myself from the doorway and went through the small store to sit in one of the desk chairs next to the reception desk and wait for Claire while she told them they could learn more about the American Revolution in one of the other galleries.

Before long Claire joined me behind the desk.

"You certainly got their attention," I said to her as she settled in.

She smiled contentedly. Claire loved to share all things Monroe with the museum's visitors. Well, most things Monroe. Since she'd been hired as a guide at the museum, we'd been having ongoing conversations concerning the contradictions in the lives of Monroe and other Founding Fathers. They fought for freedom and spoke of equality and yet were enslavers. The contradiction presented a lot of challenges, as well as opportunities for discussion for Claire, her family, and the staff at the museum. History was a fascination of hers, and those contradictions were something any historian or history buff had to wrestle with.

Despite the contradictions, she was in her element when she was at work.

"Do you have time to wait? I can't go outside with the visitors in here until Marie arrives. She should be here soon, though."

On weekdays, one guide was on duty to open the museum at ten a.m. At noon, a second guide came in for the afternoon. Having had many lunches with Claire over the years, I knew the guides either spent most of their day orienting visitors to the museum or sitting quietly reading or watching things online on the computer behind the reception desk depending on the time of year. Visitation increased dramatically during the summer, around spring break, and when the snowbirds were traveling to or from Florida. With downtown Fredericksburg three miles off of Interstate 95, it was a convenient place to break up the journey with a variety of restaurants to choose from, museums, Civil War battlefields, and a couple hotels and B&Bs if they wanted to spend the night.

"Sure, I can wait. I need to meet up with Jane at the police station at two, so, I've still got plenty of time," I said.

"More about the break-in? Did they arrest someone?"

"Not as far as I know. Detective Gomez probably wants to ask us some more questions. Jane didn't say. She just texted me and told me I needed to be there. I doubt it will take long. What else can she have to ask us? I wasn't involved at all. I was only there for moral support for Jane."

"She might need you to sign a statement," offered Claire. "You have to promise to call me as soon as you leave if they've found a suspect."

I opened my mouth to promise her but stopped as the sound of footsteps echoed up the stairs leading to the basement archives. I swiveled slightly so I could see who it was and smiled at Mark Murray, the museum's curator, coming up the steps.

The space where I was sitting was situated to the left of the reception desk and between the top of the basement stairs and the door to the sole public restroom in the museum. So, I had to scoot my chair out of the way to allow room for Mark to move past me after he opened the latch on the wooden gate at the top of the stairs.

We greeted each other with smiles. He was a quiet, kind but reserved Caucasian man in his early 40s, with short, spiky, thick black hair. From what I knew of him he was soft-spoken, smart, and single. The last fact was one Claire reminded me of from time to time in what she thought was a casual way, but he was a bit young for me. Jane was more the cougar type.

When Mark first started his job at JMM, Claire had heard through the museum grapevine he'd grown up in the area and was married for a few years in his early 20s but had remained a committed bachelor since their divorce. He wore standard business casual khakis with a pale lavender button-down shirt and a vibrantly violet tie.

"Good morning," I said while scooting my chair over a little more.

"Good morning, Liv. It's good to see you. Has Claire been able to recruit you as a guide yet?" He smiled kindly at Claire.

"No, not yet, but she's still trying. Maybe one of these days I'll give in."

"If you do, we'd love to have you join us." He leaned against the reception desk. After a hesitation he asked, "Did I hear you say a suspect has been found in relation to the break-in?"

That's how things are in Fredericksburg. It's a small enough community you didn't have to specify which break-in. It's not like there was a rash of high-profile robberies in the area.

"The door was open downstairs." He shrugged. "You know how sound travels down the stairwell," he said to Claire.

She nodded in reply. The museum's guides had been embarrassed several times by the topics of conversations they thought were private, only to find Mark climbing the stairs soon thereafter. They told themselves he was too wrapped up in his work to take note of the woes of their relationships or friendships or town gossip. Though, I'd bet he heard more than they'd like to admit.

Claire had told me of one instance when the conversation that was overheard resulted in mild repercussions. There had been a follow-up, staff-wide memo prohibiting discussions of sexually inappropriate subject matter while on duty at the reception desk. Boy, did we have fun with it at our next Monthly. We spent most of the evening guessing what the inappropriate subject matter might have been and who it involved. Our wild conjectures ended up being more fun than the actual story had been.

I realized Mark was waiting for my response. "No. I was telling Claire I'm not aware of any progress that's been made in the case. I have to go by the police station this afternoon for a follow-up, but it's probably to take care of paperwork or something minor like that."

"I hope they catch whoever's responsible. Your friend must be pretty upset. Was much taken?"

Claire said, "No, Jane wasn't able to discover what if anything was stolen. The only thing the police—"

The family of four wandered past the store which was also the hallway leading to the desk, but the mom broke off from the others and approached us glancing around in a way that usually meant someone was in need of the restroom.

"Where is the ladies' room?" she asked.

Mark gestured to the door I was blocking with my chair. I hopped up and we played the musical chairs necessary to maneuver in the small space. Mark took a few steps backwards, so I could slip past the visitor to where he had been standing in front of the desk. Then she had a clear path to the restroom. Claire stood as well and the three of us moved to the lobby in front of the entry door to give the woman some privacy, which there wasn't a lot of if the guides had to remain at the desk when other visitors were in the store.

In the midst of our exodus from the desk, Marie arrived for her shift. She set her things down and logged into the timekeeping system on the computer to sign in. The museum was still using paper time sheets less than ten years ago, and there was still a guide or two who wished they would reinstate that system.

When the visitor exited the bathroom, she stopped to talk to Claire.

"Thank you for reaching out to our sons. It can be hard to engage them with history, but you managed it." She smiled genuinely at Claire.

"It's my pleasure," Claire replied.

"I have a question. I read it was a common practice at the time for personal letters to be disposed of after someone's death. Was that true for the Monroes?"

Claire responded. "Yes, unfortunately."

Mark joined in, offering his hand to the visitor by way of introduction. "I'm Mark Murray, curator here at the museum. You're right, it was a common practice to burn personal correspondence. While it was normal to keep letters written to friends and even family, it was common to burn letters between spouses upon the death of one of them. So, after Elizabeth died, James Monroe burned all their personal correspondence, leaving no details of their relationship for posterity."

Claire added, "All the staff here harbor a wish a secret stash of letters between James and Elizabeth Monroe will be discovered in an attic or behind a painting."

"Just like in the Antiques Roadshow," the visitor added with a smile.

"Yes, it would be quite a find," Mark said. "It was fairly common for men and women who were friends to have correspondence. For instance, George Washington and Elizabeth Powel or Abigail Adams and Thomas Jefferson wrote to each other frequently."

"It would be fun to have those letters between the Monroes, though," said the visitor.

"Yes, it would provide a glimpse into both their relationship and the daily workings of their life during the time period. But those letters were lost long ago to Monroe's grief following

Elizabeth's death. He lived one more year after her passing," Mark said.

The woman's husband peeked around the corner at the end of the store.

Seeing him, she said, "Thank you for the information," and rejoined her family.

Mark walked to another set of stairs beside the main entrance. They led up to the offices and galley kitchen on the second floor.

"Good luck at the police station," he said and climbed the stairs.

Marie tilted her head inquisitively at the mention of the police, but Claire went right into giving her an update on how the morning had been and how many visitors were currently in the museum as I gathered my things together and got out of their way.

Claire told Marie we were going to eat in the garden and went upstairs to get her food. I chatted with Marie until Claire had retrieved her insulated cooler bag.

We stepped outside into the spring sunshine. It was nice to see the leaves emerging on the trees and feel the softness in the air, as opposed to winter's bite.

Approximately half of the museum's enclosed garden area is a brick patio covered by a tent from spring through late fall. As long as the tent is up, they keep outdoor tables and chairs set up underneath it for visitors and staff to use. They get more use by staff than visitors most of the time, which is a shame since it's a lovely spot for a meal.

The museum hosts outdoor events in the garden and it's available to rent for small weddings or family parties. A chandelier hangs from the middle of the tent, providing light for evening events. Some of the Monthly ladies and I have joined in for the History Trivia Nights and my personal favorite, the Sketchy History game nights. Sketchy History is basically Pictionary using historic people and events. Trust me, it can be a challenge to draw things like the Battle of Trenton or Benedict Arnold. The cash bar at the events helps keep things light and helps encourage attendance from our circle of friends.

The remainder of the garden is either grassy or beds filled with boxwoods and a couple of rosebushes. Tucked in between two of the rosebushes is a bronze bust of James Monroe, keeping watch over the visitors coming and going. The grassy area is presided over by the gorgeous crepe myrtle. It's a type of tree I've always loved, with its smooth, mottled bark and abundant summer blossoms. This one offers a profusion of deep fuchsia blooms every summer that take my breath away.

Six- or seven-foot-high brick walls enclose two sides of the garden. The rest is enclosed by the exterior walls of the museum buildings. One exterior wall is fronted by beds of the boxwoods interrupted only by a second red door. Along the other exterior brick wall of the museum there are three wooden benches set between the windows. Above them, four dormers with windows for the upstairs offices faced out over the garden from the second floor.

While Claire and I each had on light sweaters, we weren't convinced they would be enough to keep us warm under the tent out of reach of the sun's rays, so we opted to sit on the benches in the sunshine. We wouldn't have tables there, but the brick walls we leaned against absorbed the sun's warmth and radiated it back out, making it the perfect spot.

As we ate, Claire started to tell me about a new exhibit the museum was planning. It would explore the books they have in their collection that belonged to James Monroe.

"Shit! Shit! Double shit!" I said, perhaps more loudly than I should have while sitting in the museum's garden. Thank goodness no visitors had entered the garden at that moment.

"You don't have to come to the exhibit if you don't want to," Claire laughed.

Realizing how it sounded from her perspective, I laughed with her.

"I'm sorry. As soon as you mentioned books, I remembered Sophie left two books for you at my place on Friday. She meant to give them to you but forgot, and now I've forgotten too. She wanted you to show them to Ethan."

"Why?"

"She said they were from the early 1800s. She didn't say they were related to the Monroes specifically, just that they might be of interest. She made me promise to get them to you. I'm surprised she didn't follow up with you about them herself, but all the excitement this week might have put it out of her mind. They were in a box of books left to the library in someone's will.

I set them aside after Sophie left and haven't thought of them since."

"You do have the most amazing ability to walk right past something and not see it."

It was true. I was notorious for letting things stack up. Once I put them down, I had an uncanny ability to not see them anymore. Living alone means it's not as big of a problem as it used to be. I don't mind the stacks, and all my friends are tolerant of this special trait. I did at least try while Nate was alive because he couldn't stand the stacks of things around the house. He ignored it in my workspace, though, meaning I could let my stacks run wild there.

"I'm sorry. I promise I will find them when I get home and bring them by to you later in the week."

"You could wait until next month's dinner," Claire suggested.

"Sophie is bound to disapprove of that. She was disappointed enough having forgotten to give them to you herself."

"Well then, it may not thrill you to know Sophie decided to join us for our walk later."

"Crap." Claire smiled, and I rushed on. "It's not that I don't want to see Sophie, it's just I promised her I would get them to you this week. When are you working next?"

"Normally I'd be here Friday, but someone asked me to swap a shift, so I was here yesterday instead. I won't be in again until Sunday."

"OK, I'll drop by on Sunday, and hope Soph doesn't ask about them."

We sat in the sun, soaking up the warmth. Claire was telling me about her visit with Emma on Saturday, when the museum's director, Ethan Mathis, came out the door.

Ethan was in his mid-sixties, bald, and had gray-blue eyes with a mole at the corner of his right eye. He was around six feet tall and was quick to laugh. He smiled as he took a few steps and stood in front of us in the grass.

"It's good to see you, Liv. I take it those were your dulcet tones I heard earlier?" There was laughter playing at the corners of his mouth.

It took me a second to realize he had somehow heard my swearing when Claire and I were talking. "Oh, my gosh! You could hear me?"

He threw his head back and laughed a deep, baritone laugh. "I was near one of the windows upstairs. They say you can take the girl out of Jersey, but you can't take the Jersey out of the girl."

I felt my skin flush but laughed with him. "Why the hell would you want to?" I asked with a smile. "I am sorry, though. I'll try to keep my language to a more acceptable vocabulary in the future."

While Ethan had been the director for over twenty years now, and had grown up in the area, he went to college in New York City and was a staunch Yankees fan. With my family's love of all things Orioles, we had an ongoing friendly feud over baseball, and we'd had several debates over whose fans used more profanity.

He returned the smile. "Please do so," he said with best imitation of a posh affect. "How are the girls doing? Is Bailey's job going well?"

"They're doing fine, thanks. Yes, Bailey's been there two months already. She's getting the hang of things, but it will take time until she feels settled. It's a big institution and she has a lot to learn, but she's eager to absorb as much as she can. You know how long she's wanted to work for the Smithsonian. It's a thrill for her to be there. It was incredibly nice of you to write a letter of reference for her. She was so grateful for your help."

"I don't know if it helped, but it was my pleasure. I'm always happy to see young people excited to work in museums."

I knew this was true. Every year, the museum welcomed interns from the museum studies program at the University of Mary Washington, under whose auspices the museum falls. He's always so proud when they go on to jobs in their field.

Bailey had been a guide at JMM during her first two summer breaks from college and had recently begun working at the Smithsonian's American History Museum in the Programs and Audience Development department. She had graduated from Virginia Commonwealth University with a degree in Mass Communications and a focus on public relations. While applying for jobs in D.C., she started taking graduate level museum studies courses through George Washington University. It will take her a couple years to finish the program taking classes part-time, but she's determined.

"It's still hard for me to wrap my head around the idea that she and Steve are old enough to be out there on their own," he said.

"I know, but it's so good to see them thrive. And especially good to see them not need to move in with their parents."

We all laughed, each of us having different levels of unspoken desires to have our kids living at home again.

We'd both had kids later than the norm—Ethan's wife Melody had become unexpectedly pregnant at 40. So, despite our age difference, Ethan's son Steve and Bailey were born the same year, and in a city our size that meant they'd known one another most of their lives.

Fredericksburg has one elementary school, one upper elementary school, one middle school, and one high school. So, if you want your kids to go to public school, everyone within the city limits goes to the same schools, which means you basically spend all your life from kindergarten through high school with the same group of kids, give or take a few. That has benefits and disadvantages. If you don't get along with some of the kids, there's no escaping them by living in different districts. Cliques form, even among the parents. The only alternatives are private schools or moving to one of the surrounding counties, but that won't help avoid the cliques. I guess it's human nature to travel in packs.

Luckily, Bailey and Steve had always gotten along. They'd been friends since first grade, so I'd met Ethan long before Claire started working at the museum.

"Would you like to join us?" Claire asked Ethan, gesturing to one of the benches.

"No, thanks. I'm waiting for Mark to come down." He glanced up at Mark's office window above us. "We have a meeting on campus in fifteen minutes."

Claire offered to go upstairs to get Mark, but Ethan waved the offer aside.

Ethan barely had time to enjoy the sunshine before Mark came hurrying out the door. He'd put on a navy-blue blazer with his name tag attached to his jacket pocket.

"Sorry for the delay. I was trying to get an email sent out before we left."

Ethan said to Claire, "If you get any calls for either of us, we'll be on campus for at least an hour and a half." He nodded a farewell at me like any good gentleman would. "It was good to see you. Please give my best to Bailey."

"I will. Thanks," I said.

They waved their goodbyes and left the garden together.

CHAPTER
FOURTEEN

I left for the police station at quarter to two. The old station used to be downtown, but a new, modern station opened in 2007 between downtown and Central Park.

Yes, Fredericksburg has its own Central Park. No, it's not a beautiful, communal park space. It's a large, big-box retail development. It used to be a golf course and pastureland. It was difficult to watch as the land was filled in and paved over to make way for big stores like Walmart and Target, but it was a financial boon to the city. Nate and I had many late-night discussions about the high costs of what some call progress. I can't say I never shop there; I am imperfect, after all. However, I try to patronize the small businesses in Fredericksburg's Main Street District first and foremost. Jane would never let me forget it otherwise.

The one upside to the development there is they built a stadium for one of the minor league teams in the Washington

Nationals organization. It's fun having our own minor league team, even if they aren't associated with the Orioles.

The new police station is leaps and bounds ahead of what they used to make do with, but there was something to be said for the old location being in the heart of town, a sense of security it brought.

When I arrived, Jane was waiting for me in the parking lot beside her SUV. She started right in before I was even six feet away.

"How did you know?"

I stopped next to her, startled by the force of her question. "Know what?"

"About the box of books."

My eyes widened. I felt excited and slightly nauseous. "What did you find out?"

"There were two books missing. Luckily, I'd done a basic inventory of what was in the box. How could you possibly have known?"

The awe mixed with apprehension in her expression was what I feared and the reason I've tried not to tell anyone about the insights I'd been having. People are wary of others who might be able to see more of their lives than they would like them to. I can't say I blame them.

There's one night of my life when I wish I or someone else had been able to see into my future and warn me. It's the only thing that's made me wish my hot flashes had started earlier in my life. Then Nate might still be alive.

The weather forecast had been iffy the day he died. It was going to be slick later that night, but it shouldn't have been bad when Nate was on the road. We don't get a lot of snow in this part of Virginia. Instead, we get sleet and ice, but all that had come down so far that day was rain. There was a nor'easter off the coast, but luckily the worst of it was supposed to bypass us. Yet apparently, the storm dropped just enough precipitation and the temperature dropped just enough to be lethal.

The shift in the temperature happened quickly, probably more quickly than Nate had anticipated. One patch of black ice and he'd spun into oncoming traffic.

That's how I felt seeing Jane's reaction, like I was sliding toward danger, completely out of control.

I shrugged. "I wasn't sure. It was just a feeling. Were the books valuable?" I knew redirecting her to the books would distract her.

"One wasn't, but the other was the one out of all the books in the box that would bring the highest price. So, it must've been someone who could recognize its value."

"That has to limit the number of suspects, right? But why would they go to all that trouble to steal two books, especially when one wasn't worth much?"

"I wondered the same thing. Another odd thing was the box was taped shut."

"Why is that odd?"

"I packed the box and made the inventory list and then taped it up because I was planning to take it to the book show with me. I had noted some preliminary information about each title so I could do some research on them before I left town. Since the show was only a couple weeks away, I'd decided I would try selling them there first rather than in the store. I know a few people who will be attending who I thought might be interested in some of them. I didn't see the purpose of putting them out on display in the store first and so, I sealed it up."

I was confused. "Wait, if it was sealed when you checked it, how do you know it wasn't the tape you had put on it?"

There was an excited gleam in her eye. "When I discovered the books were missing, I thought the same thing. How could it be sealed and still have two books missing? So, I examined the box more closely to see if the tape had been ripped off and replaced and found there were two layers of tape."

She said it triumphantly, but I was still missing something, and my confusion must have showed because Jane frowned at me.

"It's not too odd for an old box to have more than one layer of tape on it, is it?" I asked.

I could see the realization hit her. "No, no, the books originally came from a variety of places. I put them all together in one brand-new box. So, there should have been one layer of tape on the box, but there were two. The first layer wasn't torn off, so they must have cut it down the middle just like I'd done when I opened it, which is why I didn't catch it at first."

My brows furrowed as I let the implications sink in. "So, whoever it was brought a roll of tape with them? Seems like a lot of planning. And good detecting on your part," I added.

She beamed at the compliment. "It was surprisingly fun." Her smile faded quickly. "Though, it *was* creepy to realize how much planning must have gone into it. I felt like someone had been watching me."

We each shuddered to shake off the unsettling thought.

"We should get inside. Detective Gomez'll be waiting for us," I said.

Jane nodded and turned in the direction of the station, but I touched her arm to stop her.

"Can we not tell Gomez about the feeling I had about the box? I mean, she'd already asked you to do an inventory of the room, right? So, there's no need to mention it, is there?"

I couldn't gauge her reaction. Was it humor or uncertainty or maybe a mixture of both?

With a half smile she said, "No problem."

We approached the station side by side. I'd read about the new building in our local paper, but luckily had never had reason to go inside. Unfortunately, I can't say the same for Mary. Her son Jamie went through a rough time after her divorce. She got him back on track, but not before she'd had to make a visit to the police station.

Jane and I entered the lobby together, passing large portraits of the chief of police and the division captains. We approached the glass-fronted office space at the far end of the lobby and rang the bell. The officer who came to greet us notified Detective Gomez of our arrival and invited us to sit on the benches we had just passed.

We hadn't been waiting long when Gomez opened a door in front of us and invited us to follow her. She led us down a hallway lined with offices and workspaces to the left and right. Partway down the hall she stopped at a door on the right and used a card to scan us into the detective division. She led us past a reception area, interview rooms, and cubicles to a door with her name on it and pushing the door open to let us in, allowed us to enter ahead of her.

"Please have a seat," she said in her brusque, yet not unkind way.

It was an office I would have to call sterile. It was all business, like Gomez. There was a desk with two dull, gray, slightly uncomfortable armchairs in front of it and plenty of space between her desk and the chairs. There were no photographs on the walls, just certifications and commendations. Several of the certifications were from the Metropolitan Police Department in Washington, D.C.

"I didn't know you worked in D.C. Were you a detective there as well?" I asked.

Jane followed my line of sight to the frames on the wall.

Gomez walked around our chairs to her seat behind the desk. "Yes. I was a detective in the District for ten years prior to coming here."

I saw the amazement I felt reflected in Jane. It was a strange career choice to move from being a detective in a big city to being one in a significantly smaller city. I wondered about what had precipitated the change, and briefly considered asking her.

I could tell the question would not be a welcome one, which only made me more curious about her.

She cleared her throat and started right in. "I have a few follow-up questions, mostly for you, Ms. Harper. First, were you able to take an inventory of the book room?"

Jane invited Detective Gomez to call her Jane, which she never did as far as I know, and proceeded to update her on what she had discovered when she inspected the box, leaving me out of it entirely. The detective nodded and took notes.

"You're certain there was no tape on the box when you taped it closed the first time?"

Jane replied without hesitation. "I'm positive. It was a brand-new box. I'd just received a shipment of them. I had to order some sturdy ones for the book show, so it had never been used."

Gomez's eyebrows drew together, and lines showed on her forehead. "That is odd. Whoever it was thought enough about it, or knew enough about your procedures, to bring packing tape with them."

I couldn't help but chime in. "It is odd, isn't it? What kind of person would've thought of bringing tape? What would the purpose of it be? Why not leave it unsealed? It's not like it would disguise there'd been a break-in, with the alarm going off."

Her gaze shifted between the two of us eventually resting on Jane. "And only two books were stolen? What would you estimate the worth of those books to be?"

Her attention had returned to her notebook, pen at the ready for Jane's answer.

"One was worth very little. However, the other was a copy of Jane Austen's *Pride and Prejudice.*"

"*Pride and Prejudice.* Why would that be valuable?" inquired Gomez.

I wasn't sure if her skepticism was tainted with an anti-romance cynicism, but I let myself imagine it was. She didn't wear a wedding ring, and it fit nicely with the backstory I was creating for her in my mind.

I could hear Jane's love of old books and the mysteries revealed by them in the tone of her voice. "So much depends on the edition, and the condition it's in, whether it's signed by anyone, what the cover is made of, things like that. I hadn't had time to dig into its history yet, but its publication date of 1848 was enough to raise my hopes."

"Dig into its history?" Gomez questioned.

"Yes, if there is a bookplate or a handwritten dedication traceable to a person of note, it can increase the value exponentially. A first edition of *Pride and Prejudice* sold at auction not long ago for $100,000."

Gomez's pen hung suspended over her notepad. "For one book?"

"It was a first edition," said Jane with enthusiasm. "It's a piece of literary history."

Gomez looked skeptical. It was like watching a tennis match with my head moving back and forth between them.

"And the copy you had. Would it have been worth that much?"

"I wish, but no, it wasn't a first edition. Its publication date was too late, but it still could potentially be worth $2,000-$3,000. I was excited to research it. I could kick myself for not taking pictures. I do it with all the rare books for insurance purposes and for the website, but I hadn't done it yet."

"Are those new books covered under your insurance?" Gomez's tone was light, but she was clearly on the alert for a possible motive.

"Yes and no. Technically they would be, but I would have a hard time filing a claim for the potential value with no photos of the stolen books, particularly the copy of *Pride and Prejudice*. I have no evidence it was a rare edition, so I can't prove what it might have been worth."

She paused, thinking. "That's what I keep coming back to. Whoever stole it must have had some idea of how to appraise a book."

"Why's that?" asked Gomez.

"There were a bunch of other books in the box, some with publication dates around the same time. Whoever it was stole the most valuable one."

Gomez perked up. "And would your average person know that?"

Jane turned to me, and I felt Gomez turn to me too.

"What? I'm supposed to be the average person?"

"Average when it comes to appraising rare books," Jane replied.

I shrugged. "Thanks for the clarification." I let the sarcasm hang in the air momentarily. "Other than what I've learned over the years from you, yes, I might be considered average in that regard. I mean if I came across a copy of *Pride and Prejudice* and it had a publication date in the 1800s, I would know enough to bring it to you, but I wouldn't have a clue what it might be worth."

I had apparently proven Jane's point, because she shifted her focus to the detective.

There was amusement in Gomez's eyes as she took in the two of us.

"And the other book? You said it would have sold for very little. Any idea why someone would have stolen that one?"

"No, it's odd. It was a copy of Dickens's *A Christmas Carol*. It was an older edition, but not old enough to be valuable."

"Was there anything unique about it?"

"Nothing special. It had someone's name written on the inside. I assumed it was the owner's name, but it wasn't a name I recognized."

This interested Gomez. "Do you remember the name?"

Jane paused, thinking. "Not off the top of my head. I planned to research it later because it wasn't anyone noteworthy as far as I knew. Do you think it could be relevant?"

"Someone took that book for a reason, so it could be important. Would you would have noted it in your inventory list?"

"Most likely. I can check and get back to you. It would have been in the pictures of the books if I had gotten around to it."

"Please let me know if you did write down the name," Gomez said and then shifted gears. "So, it must be someone who has some knowledge of rare books. What about other antiques dealers in the area? Do you have any competitors who might have a grudge against you or who are in financial trouble?"

This question was the only one to silence Jane. Since I knew her so well, I could see the wheels turning in her mind, but I'd have been surprised if the detective's honed instincts hadn't picked up on it too. There could be fierce competition between some of the dealers, but I knew they were a fairly close-knit group. While they were always suspicious of any new dealers who wanted to get a foothold in the local market, I couldn't imagine Jane would call anyone out as a suspect.

"No one in particular," was Jane's attempt at avoiding the question.

Gomez persisted. "Meaning there's no one you know of or meaning everyone could fall into one of those categories?"

Jane shrugged. "I can't honestly say I know the financial situation of all the other dealers. There are a couple I'm more competitive with in terms of sales, but no one I'd say might break into my store. And I keep returning to the question of why. The only thing that makes sense is they must have been there for a specific item."

Gomez made a few notes on her pad.

I should have kept my mouth shut, but that's not really my specialty. "What about the people at the library book sales?" I asked and found Jane scowling at me.

It was too late. It had already drawn Gomez's interest.

"What book sales?"

I could still feel Jane's disapproving eyes boring into me as I redirected my gaze to Gomez. It hit me all at once that I could get Sophie into trouble if I mentioned she regularly set books aside for Jane prior to the sales. So, I carefully worded my response.

"It's probably not a big deal, but they have used book sales at the library. I've been to them a few times and noticed they have a security guard or two stationed around the lobby. It struck me as odd."

"You said 'the people' at the book sales. Who did you mean?"

Jane came to my rescue. "I told her about it." The detective's attention moved to Jane. "They started hiring security guards a few years ago when a couple people got a little aggressive about getting to the best books first."

"People get aggressive at library book sales?" She seemed torn between skepticism and laughter but focusing on the facts won out. "The best books. What do you mean by that?" Gomez's eyes were intent on Jane.

"The ones with the most potential value. Look, detective, as you know, it's a small town in a lot of ways. If there's someone with a long, local family history or who has an especially valuable estate going up for auction, all the antique dealers and even flea market vendors hear about it beforehand. We tend to circle a bit like vultures trying to get to the most valuable pieces first."

Both of Gomez's eyebrows rose this time at her choice of words, and Jane went quickly on.

"It's not that we're being insensitive to the family. We're all trying to make a living selling antiques and the truly valuable or good quality pieces don't come on the market every day. If you get there last, you'll get what won't last is the mantra we live by. It's just how it works."

"So, how does that relate to the library book sales?"

"Occasionally someone who supports the library will stipulate in their will that their book collection should go to the library to help them raise funds rather than be sold at auction."

"And so, there's competition for those that do make it to the sales?" Gomez asked.

"Yes, because it levels the playing field. The prices are incredibly low compared to an auction and if you get to a book first, it's yours. No one can outbid you. But after one of the older volunteers got knocked down a few years ago, they started having security on the first day of the sales."

Gomez made a couple notes, then continued. "Do you know the names of the people who were involved?"

Jane hesitated. "No, I didn't witness the incident."

"I thought you attended these sales?"

"I go sometimes, but I often send Ellie."

Gomez flipped through her notes. "Eleanor Davis? Your assistant manager?"

"Yes."

"Would she have been there when the volunteer was knocked down?"

Jane was getting more and more reluctant. "I don't remember."

"I see. I'll follow up with her and the library on that. But you honestly don't know of any other dealers who might be bitter over a sale or who are in dire financial circumstances?" There was doubt in her tone.

I saw some memory flicker in Jane's eyes.

"I suppose there is someone who might have a reason to hold a grudge against me, but I haven't heard from him for years."

She had Gomez's interest.

"It's not someone who has a store here anymore, and that was kind of thanks to me. But there is no reason for me to believe he would've done this. I've had no contact with him since we had a falling out."

"What kind of falling out?"

Jane sounded exasperated. "Detective, someone has broken into my store. Luckily, no one was hurt and only a couple items were stolen. The last thing I want to do is dredge up the past in a way that would dredge up animosity toward me and most likely for no good reason. I'd rather let sleeping dogs lie. I mean, how does this work? Do I have to pursue this or press charges in this kind of case?"

"Ms. Harper, I understand your reluctance. It's common for victims of crime to want to forget the whole thing. Many people are frightened by the thought of having to face someone who's harmed them. But if we ignore this and they try it again in your store or someone else's, people could get hurt next time."

"Next time? You think they might try again?" Jane asked anxiously.

I reached out and put my hand on her arm.

"Why would they do that?"

Gomez hesitated, trying to decide how much to say. "It doesn't feel plausible that someone would go to the trouble of obtaining your security code and hiding out in the store for one book worth a couple thousand dollars and another with almost no value at all."

"Doesn't *feel* plausible?" I couldn't help asking. It was the first time she talked about a feeling rather than logic and facts.

Gomez ignored me. "Based on what we've found so far, I agree, it appears they were after something more valuable, and if they were determined to get it, but didn't find it, they might make another attempt if they're convinced it's still in your possession."

Jane and I looked at each other and back at Gomez. No doubt she could see neither of us had considered this possibility.

Jane, who had been sitting up straight in her chair until now, drooped with concern. "I hadn't thought of that."

"It's my job to think of things like that and to find whoever did this." She held Jane's eyes. "And my job is substantially more difficult if you won't give me details regarding potential suspects, and someone who lost their store because of you has to be a person of interest from my perspective."

Jane gave in. "It was probably four or five years ago now. His name is Lawrence Macmillan Jones."

"That's quite a mouthful," Gomez said.

"Appropriate, since he was quite a handful. And I'm not the only one he had issues with."

"But you said you were the reason he lost his store? What happened?" Gomez pressed.

"Well, it's probably more accurate to say I was the last straw." Jane gripped the arms of the chair, physically bracing herself to dredge up the past. "Lawrence sold plenty of legitimate pieces, but a lot of store owners, myself included, had suspicions he passed off some less than genuine items to customers who weren't knowledgeable about antiques."

"What made you think that?"

"It's fairly common to drop into someone else's store, or to ask another dealer to look at what we've acquired if it falls under their area of expertise. For instance, other dealers occasionally want my opinion on a book they've come across. After Lawrence's store had been open for a year or so, we noticed he never asked anyone about new furniture he'd acquired and wasn't overly welcoming when another dealer would drop by."

"And you'd discussed it with other store owners?"

"Yes, it came up with a couple of them."

"Did you ever go into his store?"

"I went there a few times."

"And what did you find?"

A sigh escaped from Jane. "I never went there to try to undermine him. However, when I was in the store one time, an acquaintance of mine was there. She was standing beside a sizable sideboard and when she saw me talking with Lawrence, she called me over. I tried to end my conversation with Lawrence before going over to her, but he followed me. She showed me the sideboard and asked me what I thought.

"Normally, I wouldn't comment on anything in another dealer's store, especially with them standing right there, but she was a repeat customer of mine and is influential around town. I knew if I didn't tell her the truth, it could hurt my business." Obviously uncomfortable, Jane glanced at her hands, then up at Gomez. "It was a tough position to be in, but I didn't feel like I had a choice. I could tell by looking at it that it was a reproduction."

"You could tell just by looking at it?" Gomez asked.

"When you've been doing this as long as I have, it's pretty easy to tell. However, I opened the drawers to confirm my suspicions. The joints on the corners of a drawer can tell you a lot about a piece of furniture. And then I saw the price tag. It said it was from the early 1900s and he was asking seventeen hundred for it, which would have been a little high even if it had been a period piece, but for a reproduction was way too high."

"What did you say?" I asked, so enthralled by the story I had forgotten all about Gomez.

"I didn't say anything. I just hesitated. I knew she could afford the price and I could have simply smiled and said it was lovely. She might not have decided to buy it either way. But my store is my livelihood, and I couldn't risk her wrath and losing her and her friends as customers if she found out I had let her buy what she thought was a legitimate antique. My hesitation was all the information she needed."

"Did she direct her wrath to Mr. Macmillan Jones?" asked Gomez.

"She didn't say anything to him in the store that day. She took my arm and walked me to the door. I got the impression she'd realized the predicament she'd put me in. If looks could kill, I would've been dead based on how he glared at me when she and I left together. I got an angry call from him later in the day. But I told him he wouldn't have had a problem if he hadn't been trying to sell reproductions as period pieces. It was an uncomfortable conversation, but as far as I was concerned that was the end of it."

"It wasn't?" asked Gomez.

"No. The same woman came by my store later in the week and asked me for more details on the sideboard. She'd been making inquiries about Lawrence and his store and asked some pointed questions. So, I told her what I'd seen, and my opinion based on my observations. She spread the word around pretty fast, and it wasn't long before he didn't have any customers except for tourists. That's when I received an irate phone call from him."

I had a memory of Jane telling us about the call at one of our Monthlies. She was pretty shaken up by it, but I remembered admiring her for being strong in the face of his anger.

"Was he threatening?" Gomez asked.

"He was more insulting than threatening, but he said he was going to have to close his store and it was all my fault. I reminded him not so gently it wasn't me who made him try to scam people. He called me a bitch for around the tenth time and hung up."

"And you never heard from him again?"

"No. Though I've found a few critical reviews posted online about my store that I couldn't link to any legitimate purchase. I've wondered once or twice if he posted them, but I have no proof, and I've never seen him or been contacted by him since then."

"Do you know if he opened another store somewhere else?"

"Not that I'm aware of, but I had no desire to keep up with him."

"And you haven't heard of him being seen around town?"

Jane shook her head. "No, thank goodness."

Gomez flipped through her notes. "Was he living here when the problems occurred at the library book sales?"

Jane paused, reflecting on the question and the time period. "He might have been here at the time. I don't have any idea when he left compared to when the sales were."

"We'll see what we can find on him," said Gomez. She seemed to get lost in her own thoughts momentarily. "The nature of the crime does suggest the thief was searching for something in particular. Can you think of nothing of substantial value someone might have known was in the store?"

Jane pondered the question before responding. "My first instinct would be jewelry. There's nothing overly expensive on its own, but if you put them together, it would add up. Yet whoever it was didn't even touch the jewelry. From what I can tell, they were only interested in the books."

"Yes, that's been my conclusion as well. The jewelry cabinet didn't show signs of tampering. I believe they were expecting to find a specific item. Where did the books in that box come from? Were they all from one source?"

"No. There were books from several places in the box. There were a few from an online auction, a few from estate sales, some that were left to the library, and some from a couple of dealers I do business with on a regular basis. They watch out for things they know I'm interested in."

She didn't technically say she got any of the books from a sale at the library, but the detective must not have taken note of the wording because she pursued another line of questioning.

"Would people participating in online auctions know who you were?"

"No, we only see each other as paddle numbers for the auctions. It's anonymous. On rare occasions auctioneers may reach out to a buyer afterwards to see if they're willing to be contacted by someone else who'd been interested in the piece they purchased, but no one followed up with me on any of these books."

"And the dealers? Is there any chance one of them might be sorry they sold you a book and want it back?"

"It's not likely with the caliber of people I work with. They will have done the research on their end before selling it to ensure they can get the best price. They wouldn't miss a book with real value," Jane said.

Gomez was thoughtful for a moment. "So, the price is based on whether it's a first or special edition, the publication date, what else?"

"It depends on so many things. What's hot in terms of collectors at any given time. The condition of the book, whether the binding is broken, the foxing on the pages, the quality of the paper, whether it's signed by the author or an illustrator, or if it has a handwritten dedication from someone prominent. There are many factors."

"Foxing?"

"It's when the paper starts to deteriorate and develops spots or starts to brown." Jane explained.

"Is there anything else that might make it valuable other than the standard things?"

Gomez was thorough, I'll give her that. Jane pondered the question in silence.

"For instance, could anything be hidden in one of the books?" suggested Gomez.

Jane smiled a little. "That only happens in movies. I've never come across a book with a hidden map or treasure."

"But is it something you look for?"

"Generally, it's standard to flip through a book in case anything was tucked between the pages for safekeeping, like family photos, money, letters, that kind of thing, and in rare instances people will use book safes. However, hidden items or book safes are uncommon and even if found, aren't usually worth much on their own. Though they can help increase the resale price of the book minimally."

"Where did you purchase the copy of *Pride and Prejudice*?"

"It was in a box of books I bought through an online auction. It was a pretty good find. I was excited about it."

"A find? You didn't know what was in the box when you bought it?"

"No. It's fairly common with a large estate for books to be boxed up and sold as is. It can be part of the fun of estate sales, finding one valuable object among the junk. But it can be a risk too. You might end up with a box full of cookbooks and romance novels."

"What was the name of the auction company you bought that box from?" Gomez wrote the name in her notebook. "Maybe someone in the family regretted selling the copy of *Pride and Prejudice*." She paused, flipping through her notes and contemplating the information Jane had given her so far. "And the copy of *A Christmas Carol*, where did you get that?"

"I'm pretty sure I got it through the library."

Again, I noted Jane didn't say she bought it from the library.

"Do you recall when you purchased it?"

"I don't remember exactly, but sometime within the past few months."

"I'll follow up with the library to see who's made donations recently," Gomez said. "OK. We've covered everything except the possibility of it being a current or former employee."

Gomez flipped to a new page in her notebook. "You've indicated you think it's unlikely to be a current employee."

It wasn't a question, but she waited for Jane to respond.

"Yes, I'm certain it couldn't be an employee."

"Why?" inquired Gomez.

"Mainly because all the employees know the security cameras are there to deter shoplifting, not for recording. So, they would've known they didn't need to black out the cameras."

"I considered that, but it doesn't rule them out entirely. They could have unknowingly tipped off a friend about a valuable item in the store. Or it could be a former employee. That occurs more frequently than you might imagine. Do you have any former employees who might be disgruntled and who worked there prior to the cameras being installed?"

Jane's voice expressed her weariness. "Disgruntled? No, I haven't had—" She stopped mid-sentence.

"Yes?" Gomez prompted, leaning forward slightly.

Jane hesitated but continued after a lingering pause.

"There was one employee who left on less-than-ideal terms."

CHAPTER FIFTEEN

I had no idea who Jane meant, which Gomez must have read on my face.

"Define less-than-ideal," she said.

Jane sighed, resigned. "There was a young man who worked for me who I had a brief affair with." Her eyes darted to mine.

"What?" I exclaimed. I was more shocked by not having heard about it before than by it being a young man.

Gomez tapped her pen on the surface of desk, either to get our attention or out of amusement. "How brief?" she asked.

"Six weeks or so," Jane replied.

"Who was it?" I knew I shouldn't have asked, but I was intrigued.

She glared at me momentarily, but then turned to the detective. "Since you will also insist on knowing"—she stressed the word *also*—"his name was Spencer."

She didn't share his last name, but Gomez just waited patiently, and Jane had no choice but to give in.

"Spencer Minor."

"Spencer Minor." I said it quietly without thinking and found Jane and Gomez watching me.

"Do you know him?" Gomez asked.

"No, but the name Minor rings a bell."

Jane gave me another withering stare before we both focused on Gomez, who had not missed the exchange. She looked inquisitively at Jane.

Jane slumped even more. "The Minor family is fairly well-known in Fredericksburg and shows up throughout the town's history. Their family tree is tangled with the Maury's'."

That's when I remembered the name Minor had come up at one of the trivia nights at the museum when the topic was local history. She was right about the tangled part. The two families had a very public falling out a few generations ago if my memory of it was accurate.

"As in the Maury School?" Gomez asked, referring to the original high school building downtown. It was built in 1920 and had been renovated and converted into condos, though the adjoining field and stadium seating were still used for sporting events for James Monroe High School.

"Yes," was all Jane said.

Gomez made note of it in her notebook and refocused her questions on the relationship. "Who ended the affair?"

"I did. He'd recently graduated from college, and I realized how foolish it was, despite—" she stopped herself, blushing.

"Despite what?" asked Gomez.

Jane was studying her hands clasped in her lap. "Despite how enjoyable it was at first." She reluctantly lifted her eyes to meet Gomez's. "It didn't take me long to recognize he was too young and too needy."

"Needy in what way?"

"He started calling me at the store on his days off and texting me at all hours. Despite our age difference, he was more interested in it becoming a serious relationship than I was. He even began to act like it gave him seniority over some of the other employees. I could tell it was going in a direction that wouldn't be good for me or the store, so I ended the relationship." Once she'd started, the words kept coming. "I hadn't planned to fire him. I hoped we could get past it, but it didn't seem to be possible."

"Why's that?"

"He kept on texting and calling me night and day, wanting to talk about what went wrong and telling me we could work it out. His insistence we could work it out concerned me. On top of all that, he'd become erratic about showing up for his shifts at the store." She paused.

"So, what did you do?" Gomez prompted.

"I was worried I'd need to fire him but wasn't sure how to handle it since we'd been in a relationship, however brief. So, I consulted a lawyer to find out if I could let him go without legal implications. She said my best option legally was to have his absences and any other work-related irregularities documented over a couple weeks, preferably by my assistant manager. Then we could review whether I had sufficient grounds for letting him go."

"And I presume you had sufficient grounds."

"Yes," was Jane's only reply.

"Did you give him the news yourself?"

Jane nodded her assent and said, "But I had Ellie sit in on the meeting with me at the suggestion of my lawyer." Her discomfort was evident.

"And how did he take it?"

"It couldn't have surprised him by that point. I'd stopped taking his calls and we'd given him an official warning for his absences." She looked as though she wished that would be enough, but Gomez simply nodded. "He didn't say a lot during the meeting, but as he got up to leave, he told me I hadn't heard the end of it."

"Did he say it threateningly?"

"Not really. But he called me the same evening and left an angry voice mail saying he was going to sue me for wrongful termination."

"Did you respond?"

"I sent him an email from my business address documenting the reasons he was fired and referred him to my attorney for any further questions. We didn't have any contact after that."

"No texts or phone calls? No response to the email?" asked Gomez.

"Nothing. I was relieved for the whole thing to be over with."

"Did you keep the voice mail threatening to sue you?"

"I kept it for a while but deleted it when I hadn't heard anything more from him."

"It would be helpful to have if he is involved in some way."

"My lawyer should have notes from our appointments. She might have even transcribed his message. I don't recall all the details. It was rather stressful."

"I'll need to get the name of your lawyer to see if he ever followed up with her." Gomez flipped through her notes and asked, "When did all this occur?"

Jane glanced up at the ceiling, trying to access the memories. "I think it was in 2015." Her gaze returned to Gomez. "I can verify the dates for you. I do remember it was in the fall." She sounded almost wistful for a second.

Gomez nodded as she wrote. "One last question regarding that time period: were the security cameras installed before or after 2015?"

"I don't know." Her eyes drifted back to the ceiling.

Finally, she pulled out her phone and opened her email app. After a quick search, she said, "I had it installed in September, but I didn't find out right away I wasn't going to be able to use it to record. That whole fiasco unfolded over a couple weeks."

I could see the wheels turning in her mind once more, and see she was putting unseen pieces together.

"Yes, it was all happening at the same time. I remember thinking everything had been so nice and then became such a mess." Her words stopped there; sadness etched on her face.

Finally, she added, "My lawyer's name is Helen James."

"It would help smooth the way if you would let her know I'll be in touch." There was some tension in Gomez's voice, and I wondered what run-ins she'd had with lawyers in the past.

"Detective?" I'd never heard Jane speak so tentatively. "Will it be necessary for you to talk to Spencer?" She rushed on, "I was so relieved when I stopped hearing from him and was finally able to put it all behind me. I would hate to stir it up again. I'd rather not have him reminded of me at all."

"I will make some discreet inquiries. I shouldn't have to contact him unless I find there's a legitimate reason to," Gomez said, surprisingly gently.

"Will you be able to tell me in advance if you need to contact him?"

"We will have to wait and see what I find." Seeing Jane's expression, she added, "Of course, if I discover any reason to be concerned for your safety, I will be in touch immediately."

Jane sagged in her chair again.

"Please let me know if anything else occurs to you. I've taken up enough of your time. I will have all this added to your statements. You'll receive an email in the next twenty-four hours or so, asking you to sign the final version electronically. Thank you for coming by."

We stood up, relieved we were done.

As Detective Gomez guided us out through the detectives' section she said, "We're still canvassing the neighborhood and reviewing security camera footage in the area wherever we can find it. I'll be in touch if we discover anything new."

Jane's tense shoulders softened a little as we passed through the door and walked down the hallway. "Thank you, Detective Gomez. I do appreciate all the work you're doing."

Gomez held the lobby door open for us as we left.

I started to talk as soon as we got to our cars, but Jane quieted me with a raised hand.

"We will catch up later," she said.

"But how could you not—" I didn't get to finish my question.

"I don't want to discuss it. I'm exhausted and worried and wish I could forget the whole thing." There were dark circles under her eyes and lines of concern on her brow.

"I'm sorry. Why wouldn't you be tired. It's been a shitstorm of a week." I gave her a lingering hug. "If you want to talk later, call me after my walk with Claire and Sophie."

"Oh, yeah. You need to give Sophie a heads-up about Gomez since she's going to speak to someone at the library about donations that've been made," Jane reminded me.

"She, Claire, and I are meeting at the museum after Claire's done for the day. I can talk to her then." Seeing Jane's raised eyebrows, I added, "No, I'm not stalling. I will talk to her about it. And I promise not to mention Spencer."

CHAPTER SIXTEEN

Sophie and I sat at a table under the tent in the museum's garden to wait for Claire and Marie to finish closing up. I leaned in her direction, speaking quietly. "Jane and I had to go to the police station this afternoon to see the detective handling the break-in and there's something I have to tell you." Sophie perked up, interested.

I was going to continue when I saw Ethan walking through the wrought-iron gate.

He smiled and asked if he could join us. I sat up and gestured to one of the empty chairs at the table.

"To what do I owe the pleasure of seeing you twice in one day?" Ethan asked.

I smiled at his formal address. It grew out of being immersed in texts from the 1800s all the time, which was a nice way of saying he's a history nerd.

"We're waiting for Claire. We're trying to take advantage of the warmer weather and the one clear day this week to get some much-needed exercise and sunshine."

I felt like he hesitated before speaking. "Ah, from the way you were huddled, I was envisioning a more nefarious reason."

I didn't have to come up with a reason to justify our close proximity, because Claire emerged from the museum's red door and saved me from needing to explain. She had changed out of her work clothes into black Athleta leggings, an ivory, oversized crew neck sweatshirt, and sneakers.

She joined us at the table but didn't sit down. She had a specific window of time for our walk and figured that was why she remained standing.

Still, she asked, "How did things go at the police station?"

"It was fine. It took longer than I expected, but Detective Gomez mostly asked—" The ringing of my phone interrupted me. I looked and saw Jane's name.

Glancing up I said, "It's Jane."

I answered and I'm sure they could all hear her speaking, because she was obviously excited as she plunged right in.

"I'm on my way to the police station now. Gomez called. They found something on someone else's security footage."

My eyebrows shot up. "What did they find?"

She went on, her voice a higher pitch than normal. "She said they have an image of someone who might be a person of interest. They're hoping to find the same person on footage from other cameras, but unfortunately not many of the businesses have exterior security cameras that record video."

"What does she want you to do?"

"She wants me to see if I can identify the person. You know, like if it's one of the other shop owners who might be a competitor or—" she hesitated. "Or anyone else I might recognize."

I suspected she was afraid to find it might be Spencer. "You have to call me as soon as you're done."

"I will." She stopped to swear at someone in another car. When she spoke again it was with the same edge of franticness in her voice. "Keep your phone with you. I'll call you as soon as I'm done. I've got to go; I'm pulling into the parking lot now. Bye."

She didn't hear me wish her luck, because she disconnected before I could get a word out.

After I put my phone down, I found there were three eager faces waiting.

"Well?" Claire said as she pulled out a chair and sat down. "What did she say?"

"I figured you caught every word; she was so loud." I relayed the news to them without saying a word about Spencer. It wasn't my secret to tell.

"And they think it might be the thief?" asked Sophie.

"Apparently so. The detective referred to him or her as a person of interest," I replied.

"So, they don't know if the thief was male or female?" Ethan asked.

That gave me pause. "I don't know what made me say it that way, but no, as far as I know they can't be sure. In my mind, I'd been assuming all along it was a man, when it could just as easily have been a woman."

"How sexist of you," said Sophie, crossing her arms.

"Me, sexist?"

"Why wouldn't you think a woman could have done it? It must have taken a fair amount of planning and intelligence."

"That definitely rules out some of the men in this town," smirked Claire.

"I take exception to that, madam," Ethan retorted with a smile. "Though perhaps it is telling about your opinion of men, Liv."

I would have protested, but there was some truth to what he said. Other than my dear Nate, I had a tendency to have a low opinion of the merits of the opposite sex as a starting point when meeting one. "I stand corrected. I will henceforth be equally suspicious of men and women."

"Excellent!" said Ethan standing up. "My work here is done. Enjoy your walk, ladies. Please tell Jane I hope they find the culprit, of whatever gender." He smiled and strode toward the building as we all wished him a good evening.

We took that as our cue, pushed back our chairs and left the garden.

We walked the half block to the corner of Charles and George streets and made a right. Most of the museum guides parked on George Street when possible, where the parking was not as limited during the day. If they had to park on Charles, they'd be running outside every two hours to move their car. The City takes parking enforcement seriously, having gone so far as to buy a high-tech autoChalk parking enforcement vehicle equipped with GPS and cameras that automatically record photos of vehicles and the time as the officer drives down the street.

Claire threw her things in the trunk of her car, and we headed down George Street.

"So, do you actually believe the thief is a woman?" Claire asked Sophie.

"I didn't say it was a woman. I said it could be. I was sticking up for women," Sophie declared.

"Sticking up for us by saying we can be just as criminal as men?" I asked.

"By saying we can be smarter criminals than men," she laughed.

We took another right when we reached Kenmore Avenue and debated sexism in crime the next few blocks to William St., where we had to wait for a green light before we could cross over and continue along Kenmore.

Once we'd crossed the busy street, Sophie changed the subject. "Hey, didn't you have something you wanted to tell me about your meeting with the detective this afternoon?"

"Oh, thank you for reminding me. Between Ethan arriving and Jane's call, I completely forgot. Though you're not going to be pleased with me." I peeked at her out of the corner of my eye.

"Why on earth would I be upset with you? I have nothing to do with the whole thing."

"You do in a roundabout way." I hesitated.

"Spill it," Claire chimed in.

"Detective Gomez was pumping Jane for information about other dealers who might be suspects." I began.

Sophie and Claire laughed. "Pumping her for information? Really?" Sophie said.

"No more cop shows for you," added Claire.

"OK. OK. She was asking Jane questions about the other antique dealers who are competitors or rivals of hers, and Jane said everyone is fairly civil. That reminded me of the incivility at the book sales and before I knew it, I said, what about the sales at the library?"

There was only silence as a response. It was hard to gauge their expressions since we had to watch the path in front of us as we walked. Our many tree-lined streets may be one of the beautiful aspects of Fredericksburg, but the roots pushing the cement up can make the sidewalks tricky to navigate. Between that and the lingering puddles from the week's rain, we had to watch where we were going rather than look at each other.

From what I could see though, they both appeared perplexed, which was confirmed by Sophie's question.

"How is that a problem for me?"

"At least one of the books in the box targeted by the thief was given to Jane by you, prior to the sale." I said, with emphasis on "prior to."

"Perhaps, against library policy," I concluded.

Before Sophie could respond, someone said, "On your left."

We shifted to our right into a line as two joggers ran past us with thank-yous. As I watched them move away from us, the skin at the nape of my neck prickled. I didn't have time to focus on the sensation or what it meant, though.

"I'll never understand it," said Claire watching the runners moving away ahead of us.

"Understand what?" I asked.

"How people can run wearing almost no clothes when it's cold out."

It was in the 50s, but Claire was always cold. It was a trait I frequently envied.

"It's not as cold to them," Sophie said with authority. As a librarian she could be dangerous. She knew a little about everything, and a whole lot about a whole lot of things. "People who run consistently generally have at least a slightly higher metabolism than people who are inactive. So, their average body temperature is warmer than those of us who are more sluggish."

"Who're you calling sluggish?" Claire protested and nudged Sophie with her shoulder.

Sophie continued, "Besides, if they wore more layers to start with, they'd have to take them off after they warmed up and then what would they do with them? Carry them the whole way?"

"I suppose you might have a point," Claire said, still a bit skeptical.

I slowed my pace, falling silent. I had a nagging feeling in relation to what Sophie said.

Claire called over her shoulder at me, "Come along. You don't want to be called sluggish."

I shook it off and caught up with them. "I truly hope I haven't caused any problems for you," I said, redirecting Sophie to the previous topic. "Gomez said she was going to talk to the library about recent donations and about issues they've had at the book sales."

"We have had problems at them in the past. And getting the names of donors shouldn't lead to questions around how Jane got that particular book, should it?" she asked.

"Not necessarily," I said.

"But?"

"But it depends on how attentive Gomez was. She asked Jane where she got the books in the box in question, and Jane told her they were from a variety of places, including the library."

"That's still not necessarily a problem for me."

"No, but—"

Sophie interrupted, "There are far too many buts in this conversation for my liking."

"And not enough on the courts in shorts for my liking," Claire lamented.

We were passing the tennis courts at Kenmore Park. Claire had a thing for tennis players, which I realized must've factored into our route choice. We teased her as we crossed Mary Ball Street, making our way to the canal path on the other side of Cosey Park.

"Now, back to Liv's big but," Sophie said with a grin.

I pushed her playfully. "In the course of the conversation, Jane mentioned she doesn't go to the book sales too often. She sends Ellie instead. And if Gomez asks Ellie about those books and she has no memory of them . . ." I trailed off.

"Oh. I see." Sophie became contemplative, and we continued on in silence.

As we walked up the gravel path next to Cosey Park that led to the canal path, Sophie shrugged. "If they ask me about it, they ask me about it. Nothing I can do now."

Noticing my stricken expression, she put a hand on my arm. "They wouldn't fire me for that. I have too much institutional knowledge for them to be so drastic. Besides, I know of a skeleton or two in the closets there."

Sophie had been working at the library ever since I met her eighteen years ago. You know how the story goes about the quiet, shy librarians with their hair up in buns and their glasses hiding a sinful interior? Sophie never bothered to hide it. She has a three-foot long pet ball python; she would have a Burmese python if she'd been able to talk her starter husband (as she calls him) into it. She brings it to the library occasionally to show the kids.

She's the contrarian librarian. She's as far from the soft-spoken librarian as you can get. In fact, it might do her some good to watch some videos on the art of whispering, because she has yet to master it. She laughs right out loud whether she's with friends or among the stacks. She won't hesitate to tell some kids at the library to shut up and then loudly continue a story she'd been sharing with a friend or coworker. But if those same kids have a problem, and she knows them well enough to recognize when they do, she's the first to ask them if they need help, or to listen to their troubles.

Then there was the great library coup of 2012, when Sophie's boss, who she referred to as Tyrannical Tina, was overthrown. No, I had no doubt she knew where the library's skeletons were hidden and maybe even a ghost or two.

I felt relieved by her lack of concern as we made a right onto the paved canal path. My preference would have been to go to the left so we could have followed it along the river, but we didn't have enough time. Instead, we proceeded to our right, on the portion of the trail that wanders through residential neighborhoods.

The canal path was created alongside the remnants of a mostly unsuccessful effort to make the Rappahannock River more navigable for trade in the 1800s. The canal system still holds water, and sections of the canals are aerated to avoid stagnation and its associated problems—not unlike the problems those who are more sluggish may have, I mused.

I loved walking along the canal trail. I've seen a variety of wildlife beside the canal or in its waters over the years: great blue herons, wood ducks, turtles galore, fish, osprey, beavers, green herons.

One morning I saw a turtle blocking the path that was so huge it had to have been prehistoric. I regret to this day I didn't own a cell phone at the time because everyone said I was making it up or was hung over. The turtle and I had stood staring at each other until it did a slow about-face and went down the bank into the pond on the other side of the path. I kind of liked the thought of it lurking there still, in the deeper parts of the pond, like our own Loch Ness Monster.

The ringing of my phone pulled me out of my reverie. It was Jane.

"Well?"

"So much for preliminaries," she said, a smile in her voice.

"Screw preliminaries. What did you find out? Could you tell who it was?"

Claire grabbed me by the arm and pulled me to a bench between the dog park and the path.

"I've put you on speaker so Claire and Soph can hear you," I told her.

"OK. Unfortunately, I couldn't tell who it was. The person was wearing a hooded sweatshirt when he jogged by, and the video is grainy." Jane sounded disappointed.

"Do they think it's the person who broke in?" Claire asked.

"They can't confirm it yet. They're still canvassing other businesses for video."

"So, where was the footage taken from?" I asked.

"It was a camera at Shiloh, Old Site," Jane said.

"That's not too far from the store, I guess."

The church is on Sophia Street, a half block down Caroline Street from Jane's place and another block away after you make a right on Hanover. It made sense they'd have a security camera there. For the past few years, there'd been an increase in flyers in the region with a bunch of white supremacist propaganda on them, raising concerns about vandalism to the area's churches with large African American congregations.

"He was jogging?" I asked.

"Yeah, and I thought the same thing. A jogger on Sophia Street isn't unusual."

"It's true. So, what makes them believe it's related?" I asked.

"It's the timing. The person jogs by the camera approximately six minutes after the alarm goes off."

"Doesn't that sound like a long time to get from your store to the church, especially if you're running," I said.

"Yup, my thoughts exactly, but Gomez said it's possible they couldn't just run away from the store without attracting attention. Which means if they exited through the window behind the building and had to wait for passing cars or another pedestrian, they could've been passing by the church at the time on the recording. She's had some officers downtown searching for evidence in the alleys and along the river. She got a call while I was there about a jacket they found snagged on a fallen tree in the water. She suspects the person may have planned to take cover temporarily somewhere after leaving the store before making their escape. Gomez said at the very least, even if the man or woman in the video isn't involved, they might've seen or heard something."

"So, you can't even tell if it's a man or a woman?" I asked.

Sophie and Claire were hanging on every word.

"Gomez thinks it's a man, but it's hard to tell since they only pass in front of the camera for a second."

"But couldn't they freeze the frame?" Sophie asked.

"Yes, they did, but it was still difficult to tell with the hood up. I assumed it was a man at first, but a lot of female runners are fairly flat-chested. It looked like there was a bump of some kind in that area, but it could have been the bulkiness of the sweatshirt."

There was a pause and then Jane shouted, "Nice use of the turn signal, asshole!"

A woman jogging by us on the path seemed shocked. The three of us looked at each other for a beat, then dissolved into laughter.

"Sorry," Jane said.

Knowing her like we did, we knew she was talking to us not the other driver.

"So, there wasn't anything else they discovered from the video? Nothing stood out to you? There wasn't anything familiar about the person?" I asked, trying to be subtle so Sophie and Claire wouldn't pick up on anything.

"No. It was impossible to tell who it was." I couldn't tell if she felt relieved or exasperated. "Just a person in a light-colored sweatshirt out for a run."

"I'm sorry," I said.

"I'm not sorry. I don't even care who broke in at this point. I just wish the whole thing was over with." I could hear the strain in her voice. She sighed. "On the other hand, I want them to catch the bastard and lock 'em up!"

"Now that's the Jane we know and love," said Claire.

Jane chuckled in response. "Oh, and Liv, I found I had written down the name that was inside of *A Christmas Carol*. It was Holt. The first name wasn't as easy to read, but I'd noted it began with an a. I passed it on to Gomez."

"I hope it will lead somewhere," I said.

"From your lips to— Jesus! Get the hell out of the way!—I gotta go. Bye, ladies."

We sat together, enjoying the warmth of the sun lost in our own thoughts.

Sophie broke the silence first. Turning to me, she said, "Speaking of books. Did you bring the books I gave you for Claire to the museum today?"

Remembering our talk in the garden earlier, I glanced at Claire and we both grinned.

"I take it that's a no," Sophie said.

"She did tell me about them and has sworn an oath to bring them to me on Sunday," said Claire.

I was grateful to her for coming to my defense. "I was running late this morning and completely forgot. I'm sorry. But I've already put a reminder on my phone for Sunday." I showed it to her for proof of my sincerity.

"Why are they so special, anyway?" Claire asked.

"Possibly nothing," said Sophie. "But since the time period aligned with Monroe's lifetime, I thought it might be of interest. And there was a name on the bookplate, Margaret—"

A sound behind us made her pause. We looked over our shoulders and saw a man walking quickly away from the gate of the dog park. He had what I guessed was a small collie on a leash. He was practically dragging the dog away. The setting sun was behind him. Silhouetted as he was, we couldn't see any details about him.

"Did that feel odd?" I asked.

"Kinda, though I'm not sure why," said Sophie.

"I wonder how long he was there. I didn't hear the gate squeak," I said.

The gate to the dog park always made an obnoxious noise when you opened it. I pitied the people who lived next door.

"So, it's like he didn't go in or come out."

"Was he listening to our conversation?" asked Claire.

"It's possible," Sophie said.

I knew all three of us could imagine a couple possible reasons why someone might be eavesdropping.

Sophie stood up and shook off the uneasiness. "Maybe we shouldn't discuss the break-in while we're in public." Pointing to her right, she said, "Onward."

We stood with her, and Claire said, "Jane's call slowed us down. Let's make a right on Washington and go up toward the General. I can't be late getting home. Jonathan and I have dinner plans." They were committed to having a date night at least once a month.

"The General?" I asked.

"Come on, how long have you lived here?" She lowered her voice an octave, "Brigadier General Hugh Mercer of Revolutionary War fame, of course."

"Of course," I said.

Claire ignored my sarcasm and added brightly, "Did you know General George Patton was a descendant of Hugh Mercer?"

"How would anyone know that?" I asked.

"You would if you worked at the museum," Claire said, never giving up on her campaign to recruit me.

We went right and made our way up the hill, passing the small replica of the Washington Monument—a tribute to Mary Washington, who's buried nearby. The street had at one point been called Mary Washington Avenue in her honor.

After a couple more blocks we reached the statue of the General, standing tall, sword in hand. It's difficult go anywhere downtown without passing some monument or historical marker. There's an aspect to it I find kind of sad. When you've lived here a few years and pass them every day, you don't even notice them anymore.

CHAPTER SEVENTEEN

He should never have returned, he thought as he stood beside the river watching the sun go down. He wondered if it was time to cut his losses and leave. The police were moving faster than he thought they would.

"Is it worth it?" he wondered aloud.

His only audience was his dog and two Canada geese making their way downriver. He threw a stone in their direction, missing them by several feet but provoking a disapproving squawk. Their slow drift downstream reminded him of his jacket floating away the night of the break-in.

"What if my jacket got hung up somewhere and they found it? Could they pull DNA off of it?"

He paced in a short line along the riverbank, his thoughts racing along with his pulse.

"I can't give up now. Not when I'm so close."

He envisioned the book. He pictured himself holding it, seeing Margaret's name written inside, and finding the hidden cache of letters.

None of this would be necessary if it weren't for his family name. One ugly thread woven through their family tapestry. If only his great, great, great, great aunt, a granddaughter of Margaret's, had married and changed her name. Then he might have escaped being associated with her, but instead she died with her maiden name. And so, he'd had to carry it like a weight around his neck his whole life. Born with the name of a traitor. And small towns have long memories. They don't need to remember the specifics, just one word: traitor.

There was no greater sin in the south than to be descended from someone who was considered a traitor to the "glorious cause." To this day, Betty's choices haunted him.

She had lived in a modest house on the river downstream from where he now stood, at what was the edge of the business district at the time. She'd never been married but maintained a livable income by taking in laundry. While she hadn't been an outright abolitionist, she'd been sympathetic to the plight of slaves. She wasn't outspoken about her beliefs, but everyone knew. It's probably why she never married; the number of sympathetic potential suitors would have been limited.

While the townspeople shunned her in their social circles, they would still allow her to do their washing. Eventually, she had enough work that she hired a woman, Sally, to help her with the laundry.

Sally was a black woman who lived with Betty and helped her around the house and with the laundry. Sally and her husband Dabney had been enslaved but escaped across the Rappahannock in 1863. Dabney found employment as a cook and servant for General Joseph Hooker, whose Union troops were encamped in Falmouth on the north side of the Rappahannock. Sally hadn't been able to find a job across the river, so she'd left her husband with the Union troops, surreptitiously crossed back over to find work in Fredericksburg, and found a sympathetic employer in Betty, who didn't ask questions.

Since Sally's husband Dabney had knowledge of the layout of the streets and surrounding terrain, he found he was able to provide valuable intelligence to the Union generals. Before long, he was providing precise troop movements, the location of Confederate generals, and their battle plans to General Hooker.

The way the story was handed down in his family was that Betty didn't know what was happening, didn't know Sally was providing information to her husband that she picked up from their customers. Most of the people wouldn't have paid Sally any heed when they came by to drop off their laundry. And it wasn't a stretch to imagine people would've tried to make Betty feel small by flaunting their own connections and first-hand knowledge about the war. So, they shared tidbits with her regarding the Confederate troops, and the generals, and their plans.

With the way they felt about servants and slaves, they wouldn't have thought Sally was intelligent enough to understand any of it. The joke was on them, though. Sally was listening intently to everything while doing her work.

She and Dabney had figured out a system. She would hang laundry on the lines in the yard in a specific position or sequence, which would communicate the details to him across the river. Different color shirts represented different Confederate generals or locations. When she removed a shirt, it meant a particular general had left the area. Or if she moved a shirt to a different location on the line, it indicated the direction troops were moving, to the east or west along the river. The Confederate's own dirty laundry was used against them, just like ours had been, he thought.

Confederate generals weren't the only ones baffled by the knowledge the Union leaders had of their actions. Union generals persuaded Dabney to tell them how he was obtaining such accurate intelligence.

There was never any evidence Betty was aware of what Sally had been doing. But when the story came out later in the war, in the opinion of the townspeople, embittered by their losses, she was aiding the enemy. Nothing could convince them otherwise. They stopped bringing their laundry to her, and in the end she lost her home. She was taken in by her brother and his wife nearby, but that kindness marked them as well. It was a mark that continued to be handed down from generation to generation like a birthmark. *Traitor.*

He lamented how easily a family's fortunes could change at the hands of fate. If his family was known for their connection to the Monroes instead, things would have been different. If Margaret's family had even kept the letters Elizabeth had written to her during their friendship, they would've been valuable, as there were only six letters written by Elizabeth known to have survived from the time period. But they wouldn't have been worth enough for him to be able to disappear and start a whole new life. No, it was the other letters entrusted to her by Elizabeth that were immeasurably valuable.

Those letters held the key to his future, to changing his family's luck. They could save him and his mother. He was the last male in the family line, and he took comfort in the idea it could all end with him. He had to get his hands on the music book and those letters. He couldn't run away now. He had to see it through. If he couldn't clear his family's name, he would choose a new one and start over.

And he knew where to find the book now. He hadn't set out to eavesdrop, but they had been talking so loudly he couldn't help but overhear. If he'd heard it correctly, there was a chance he could still get his hands on the book before the police could identify him. He had until Sunday to figure out how to get into her house, but it didn't give him much time for planning. He would have to improvise this time.

CHAPTER EIGHTEEN

O n Friday morning I awoke feeling a little off. Like there was something important I was forgetting.

"Caffeine might help jump-start my brain." It's never a good sign when I start talking aloud to myself. I switched on my electric kettle to make some tea. I chose a bag of black tea and dropped it into a teacup, which brought Lucia to mind. I thought of texting her, but instead considered what she would tell me to do if she knew I was feeling this way.

Seeing her image in my mind, I sat on a stool at the kitchen counter and closed my eyes. I felt the heat and tingling kick in and breathed deeply to keep myself from fighting the process.

After a couple more breaths, I was calmer, if not cooler, and let my mind wander. From somewhere there was the sound of the tinkling of a bell and I saw myself talking to Jane in her store. It came with a sense of urgency, a need to be there now.

A loud click brought my thoughts back to the kitchen. Apparently, my kettle and I reached the boiling point at the same time.

I poured the hot water over the tea bag and tried to resist the urge to leave for the store. I told myself I was letting Lucia, and the break-in, and the talk with my mom go to my head and make me think everything was a vision.

I woke up feeling off, that's all. Maybe I'm coming down with a cold.

"Honey's good for a cold," I counseled myself and added some honey to my tea. The sound of my spoon hitting the sides of the teacup as I stirred reminded me of the tinkling bell. I set the spoon down on the counter and went to my bedroom for my shoes.

I didn't check-in with Jane before going over. I worried it would seem weird to her. On my way to the store, I pondered excuses I could give for why I was there.

I needn't have worried. As soon as I entered the store, the jingling of the bell giving me goosebumps, Jane opened the door to her office and waved me over.

"I'm glad you're here. I was just about to text you."

"Why?" I asked, as she closed the office door behind me.

"Detective Gomez called. She's on her way here to give me an update." Only then did Jane pause and look at me with suspicion. "Why *are* you here?"

"It's nice to see you, too," I replied in an attempt to divert her.

She crossed her arms over her chest, holding my eyes.

Feeling the weight of her stare, I offered the lamest of the excuses I had come up with on my way there. "I was out for a walk and thought I'd stop in and see how you're doing."

"You're so full of it." She smiled and uncrossed her arms, giving me a quick hug. "Whatever the reason, I'm glad you're here."

The bell on the front door jingled again and I saw Jane's focus shift to the door with apprehension. My eyes followed hers to Detective Gomez.

She was wearing a navy FPD polo shirt similar to the one I'd seen her in previously, this time with khaki pants with a variety of pockets, bulging with the various accoutrements of a detective, and her badge on a lanyard.

It may have been my imagination, but I swear she shook her head as she took in the sight of the two of us together. She walked straight to the office door. Jane had gotten up to open it for her.

"Please come in," Jane said as she stepped backwards moving the door with her to allow space for Gomez to enter.

Jane's eyes did a sweep of the store before she closed the door. There were a few curious customers watching us. She ignored them and invited Gomez to sit down.

The detective's gaze drifted between us as she took a seat in the old ladder-back chair in front of the desk.

Jane sat behind her desk, and I took the remaining chair. Though Jane was behind the desk rather than Gomez this time, it was evident the detective was still the one controlling the conversation.

"I wasn't aware Ms. Wilde would be joining us."

"I wasn't either," said Jane evenly. "She came in right after you called."

They looked at me, and my skin flushed with heat. A quizzical expression flashed across Gomez's face before she turned to Jane.

"I'd like her to stay," said Jane without giving Gomez a chance to comment further.

The detective shrugged—or surrendered, it wasn't clear which—and got down to business. "I have some updates."

"You identified the thief?" Jane asked eagerly.

"I'm afraid not," she replied. "We made a couple interesting discoveries, though." She looked attentively at Jane, then continued. "We've located Mr. Minor."

Jane clasped her hands together on the desk in front of her as if to steady them. "Where?" she asked.

Gomez leaned slightly forward, watching Jane intently as she spoke. "Here in Fredericksburg."

"What? Here? Really?" She wasn't able to speak in complete thoughts, just rapid-fire interrogatives.

Gomez held up her hand to slow her down. "He moved to Fredericksburg from Colorado in May last year."

"He's been here for a year?" Jane's voice rose in disbelief, there was also a touch of sadness in it.

"Yes, ma'am. He accepted a job at the university and has been employed there for the past year." She paused for a beat. "You didn't know?"

"Of course not." Her knuckles grew white as she clasped her hands more tightly together, and her tone became sharper. "You're saying I lied to you about not knowing where he was?"

"As you've pointed out, it's a small community, Ms. Harper. Word travels fast. It's surprising you wouldn't know he was in town."

They weren't exactly staring at each other, but neither of them looked away either.

"If I'd known he was here, I would've told you." Jane said, breaking the stalemate, but not breaking eye contact.

Gomez nodded, apparently satisfied.

Beside her, I crossed my arms over my chest in a reflexive, defensive posture on Jane's behalf.

Gomez glanced at me with amusement and returned her attention to Jane.

"Since that gives him opportunity, we will have to confirm his whereabouts the night of the robbery. I wanted to give you fair warning before we contacted him."

"Thank you," Jane said, her voice shaky. "Can you let me know how he reacts?"

"You're concerned he'll react badly? Would it be in character for him to lash out at you in some way?" Gomez asked.

"No, I don't believe he would hurt me, at least not physically." The last part she said more to herself than Gomez, but the detective honed in on it.

"Not physically. Then what? Emotionally?"

Jane shook her head as if to return her thoughts from wherever they wandered off to. "Emotionally? Oh. No. I was thinking of the store. Like you said, word travels fast. If he wanted to, he could badmouth the store and potentially hurt my business. It's my only means of support," she said by way of explanation.

"Perhaps your silent partner can help if it comes to that," Gomez said.

Was she grinning as she shot me a side-eye?

She continued, any trace of the grin gone, "We will be as discreet in our inquiry as possible. If he gets in touch with you, please let me know."

Jane nodded her assent, unclasping her hands, clearly hoping Gomez was done.

"I also have news regarding Mr. Macmillan Jones."

Jane's eyebrows shot up. "He's not in town too?"

"No. He's in prison," Gomez said evenly.

"Prison?" It was the first time I had spoken, and a pointed glance from Jane told me it was not a good time to chime in.

"Yes, prison," Gomez said, not bothering to address me directly.

"Where? For what?" Jane's stress level was back up, as she'd reverted to short, interrogatory sentences.

"He's in a minimum-security prison in Tennessee, serving eighteen months for insurance fraud."

"Insurance fraud?" Jane's brows furrowed.

"He opened several other antique stores in different states since leaving here and had been suspected of filing false claims twice, but without sufficient evidence to convict him." She let the information sink in.

"If he's in prison he couldn't have broken into my store."

"No, he couldn't have," Gomez said, stressing the word "he."

"But?" Jane asked.

"The investigators from the insurance companies involved were going on the assumption he had a partner. He denied it, but I agree it's likely he was working with someone else."

"But why would his partner know anything about Jane?" I asked.

"They might not have. However, the first time he filed a claim was in relation to his store here in Fredericksburg. So, if he had a partner, they might've been working together for some time. It's a longshot, but we need to explore it as a possibility. Are you aware of any associates he had when he was here?"

Jane paused to consider the question. "No, no one in particular. I mean, he had employees at the store, but I don't remember meeting a partner or anyone like that."

"Did you know any of his employees?"

"Not that I recall, but I wasn't in his store more than a few times."

"We're in the process of getting their names through the store's employment records, but if he paid anyone under the table, it will make it more challenging."

Gomez pulled her notebook out of her pocket, reviewed some notes, and flipped to a blank page to write something down. Closing it again, she said, "We discovered Mr. Macmillan Jones was one of the men involved in the altercation at the library book sale you mentioned."

Jane's gaze dropped to her hands, betraying her lack of surprise.

"That doesn't appear to be news to you," said Gomez.

Jane shrugged. "I wasn't sure."

Gomez was silent, waiting for the truth.

"But I heard the rumors."

"Why didn't you tell me?"

"I wasn't convinced it was relevant because they were only rumors," Jane said, her voice trailing off, concentrating on her hands once more. "I'm sorry. I guess I should have mentioned it."

"Is there anything else you should have mentioned?" Gomez's tone was serious, bordering on accusatory.

Jane raised her head, the angle of her chin defiant. "No," was all she said.

Gomez held her eyes for a beat, and I wondered what it would be like to be interrogated by her. As soon as I had the thought, I saw myself sitting at a metal table covered in plastic in a sparse room with a bright light on the table and Gomez standing behind me.

I shook off the image and focused on Gomez, who was mid-sentence.

"—Mr. Minor today. If you hear anything of a threatening nature from him, please text or call me. However, if you believe you are in immediate danger at any point, please don't hesitate to call 911."

Jane was at a loss for words.

"There is some good news," Gomez said.

I got the impression she wanted to have something encouraging to share, which I found endearing.

"The jacket we found in the river had a can of black spray paint in an interior pocket."

Jane and I turned simultaneously toward the security cameras.

"That's where our thoughts went. We collected samples of the paint on the cameras the day of the incident. We will compare them to the paint in the can. I expect they will match. One of our technicians is examining it for fingerprints now, and we will check it for traces of DNA."

"Won't any physical evidence have been washed off in the river?" I asked.

"More evidence than you might think can be recovered from an object that's been underwater. How much depends on how long it's been in the water, and under what conditions. If what we found is linked to this crime, it hasn't been in the water long.

We're optimistic we'll find something to help us identify the perpetrator."

Jane smiled wearily.

"Do you have any questions?" Gomez asked.

"No," Jane replied.

"OK. Thank you for your time, ladies. I'll be in touch if there are any breaks in the case."

She got up from the chair and we stood with her.

"Thank you," Jane said and reached her hand out to Gomez.

They shook hands and Gomez left the store, the bell jingling behind her.

We sat down and were silent as we processed everything Gomez had shared. Jane's arms rested on the desk with her hands clasped. Her knuckles were white from the intensity of her grip.

"What is it? Are you upset about Spencer being back? Do you think it was him?"

Her eyes were glassy with tears. "I hope not. I hate that Gomez is going to have to ask him for an alibi for the night of the break-in."

Now I saw fear plainly on her face, but I misinterpreted its cause.

"Are you afraid he'd hurt you?" I asked.

"No. I don't believe he's capable of that."

"Then what are you afraid of?"

She rested her forehead in her hands. "I don't know what it is. I just feel unsettled." She lifted her head, running her fingers through her hair. "I'm freaked out someone was here in the store with me that night. I have nightmares about what would have happened if I'd discovered the thief there. I'm worried about dredging up the past with both Spencer and Lawrence. I'm tired of people's questions about the break-in."

I got up and stood beside her chair, putting my arm around her shoulder. I felt her lean into me, resting her head against my side, able to let her guard down at least a little. The people gawking in the store finally had the decency to at least pretend to shop. When she eventually pulled away, I squatted down beside her.

I was hesitant to mention what was on my mind, but I did anyway. "You sounded sad to learn he's been in town for a year without you knowing. Are you?"

The downturn of her lips and far-away expression betrayed more sadness than I would have expected, and I wondered if she'd felt more for Spencer than she'd admitted to me or herself.

She exhaled a long breath. "Truthfully, what surprised me the most, was not that he moved back without telling me, but how sad I felt when Gomez told us."

"I'm so sorry you're having to go through all this."

I was wishing I could make it all go away for her when an idea occurred to me. I couldn't make the problems go away, but maybe I could take her mind off the situation for a while, plus I didn't want her to have to be alone after the police talked to Spencer.

"Why don't I come and stay with you tonight? I can make you dinner and we can have an old-fashioned sleepover."

"You'll make dinner?" she asked with an inflection that walked the line between humor and skepticism.

"It'll be fun. We can watch a movie and drink wine and forget about the whole damn mess."

She hesitated, but then smiled. "OK. But what if I come to your place instead? It'll save me the trip into town in the morning."

"Perfect."

CHAPTER NINETEEN

It was eight o'clock by the time Jane called. She'd needed to run home after she closed the store to pack a bag and traffic had slowed her down. Traffic issues are to be expected in the region, especially on a Friday evening. There can be gridlock for miles on I-95 from the exit for Route 3 leading to Fredericksburg, all the way to Jane's exit up in Stafford and far beyond. Even the smaller roads weren't a good alternative on a Friday, and it would get worse once it was summer. The sheer number of people getting out of D.C. on the weekends during the summer could make 95 South a parking lot.

We'd already communicated about dinner plans. Jane had no desire to go out somewhere and be the target of stares and questions around the robbery. So, I'd run out to the butcher shop for two of their delicious Parmesan-encrusted chicken breasts and some wine.

I had the oven warming up, potatoes boiling in a pot, green beans ready to go into hot water, and two glasses of wine on the counter when Jane arrived.

She left her overnight bag and purse by the door and made her way into the kitchen where I was putting potatoes into a pot of boiling water. "I'm ready to put the chicken breasts in the oven." I could gauge how tired Jane was based upon her lack of questions. As my cooking instructor, she would normally have quizzed me on how I was preparing the meal. Instead, she sat on a stool at the counter and picked up one of the glasses of wine I'd poured.

"What a shitty week," she said resignedly.

I put down the fork I'd been poking the potatoes with, picked up my glass of wine, and raised it to her.

"To better weeks ahead," I said.

She raised her glass to meet mine. "Here's hoping."

We had a quiet, informal dinner sitting together at the counter. I hadn't burned anything, which helped. After dinner, I refilled our wine glasses and Jane moved to the couch, intending to pick out a movie to watch.

As I was about to sit down beside her, there was a slight creaking sound from down the hallway leading to the door.

"What was that?" Jane asked.

"I'm not sure. It's an old building, though. It creaks and groans all the time. Still, it's less noisy than our old house was." I wasn't worried, but still I asked, "Did you lock the door when you came in?"

"I don't remember locking it."

I walked down the hallway to the front door. Nothing was out of place, so I locked the door and returned to the living room.

After I plopped down the on couch, Jane said, "Thanks for not asking me about Spencer. I know you must be dying to hear about him. I would be." She laughed half-heartedly.

"I figured if you wanted to talk about it, you would," I replied.

"There's not much else to tell you. Like I said, he'd recently graduated from UMW."

"He went to UMW?"

"Didn't I say that at the police station?"

"No. You said he'd graduated recently, but not where he went."

"Huh, I could swear I did. This whole week has been kind of a blur. I've had so many conversations with so many different people." She took a sip of wine. "Yeah, he'd graduated that May, a history major. Since he was from the area, he was hanging around figuring out what he wanted to do next. He was planning to take a gap year to travel around but needed to earn some money first."

"And he thought he could earn enough working part-time in an antiques store?" I asked skeptically.

Jane laughed. "No kidding, right? He was obviously considering very low-budget travel options."

I could have left it there, but said tentatively, "It's just odd you didn't tell us. You're usually such an open book."

Her gaze fell to her hands, examining her fingernails.

"You're not typically shy about sharing your flings."

Jane had never been married, and so we lived vicariously through her adventures with various lovers and relationships.

When she looked up, she was blushing. "I was embarrassed."

I was truly shocked. "Come on. You're the least easily embarrassed person I know."

It was true. Other than in the police station when she first mentioned Spencer and right now, I swear I'd never seen her blush in all the years I'd known her.

"I know. Me embarrassed? Unbelievable, right? I mean, I knew I would get harassed since he's just a bit younger than me," she said with a grin.

"Cougar," I said.

She laughed, genuinely this time. "Exactly. That's what I knew I'd hear, but I could have taken the teasing."

Her laughter subsided and she became thoughtful. "At first, I didn't tell anyone because I really did like him and I wanted to just enjoy it. We hit it off right away when he started working at the store. I was delighted to find how much we had in common. I probably would've told you all about him if it hadn't gotten weird so fast."

She took another sip of her wine. "By then I was shocked by how immature he turned out to be and didn't know how I was going to extricate myself from it. It would've been mortifying to tell you all about it at that point."

I reached out to her. "You could've come to us. We could've helped you figure it out. I hate you went through it on your own." I paused. "And we would have at least waited until you were well out of it before we got you a cougar t-shirt."

Any gratitude she might have felt evaporated, but she smiled a little.

"This may seem like a random question, but did Spencer have a dog?" I tried to sound nonchalant.

"That is random." Her brows furrowed. "Yes, he did. He'd gotten it after graduation. I told him it was a foolish thing to do if he wanted to travel. What made you ask that?"

The text tone on her phone interrupted us. The message was long enough that she needed to unlock her phone to read the whole thing. She typed in her password, keeping it hidden from me as usual. She read through it quickly and when she closed it, another one caught her attention further down.

She said, "I completely forgot to show you this at the store this morning." She pressed on the screen and opened a text thread I could see included a picture.

"Nothing untoward, I hope," I said with mock disapproval.

She rolled her eyes and scooted closer to me on the couch. "You know I will never again show illicit photos I receive from men to any of you."

Jane had shown us some racy photos a guy named Derrick had sent her and we never let her forget it. The consensus is that's the reason she won't let any of us have the password for her phone.

"This was from Gomez. She sent me a text with the still frame from the surveillance footage so I could show it to Ellie to see if she recognized the person." She stopped and said, "Thank you for being discreet and not mentioning Spencer's name on the phone when Sophie and Claire were with you. Gomez did ask me if I thought it could be him, but I honestly couldn't say either way."

She brought the picture up full-screen and leaned nearer to show it to me. It was a grainy image of a person in a light gray sweatshirt with the hood up over their head and darker gray sweatpants.

I tried zooming in, but that did nothing but make it fuzzier. I could see what Jane meant when she said she couldn't tell if the person was a male or a female. There was a slight bump at the chest level, but I couldn't tell if it was caused by a wrinkle in the fabric or small breasts, further shrunken in a binding sports bra.

"The only thing that's beyond doubt is it's a white person," I said.

"Yes. Doesn't that help narrow it down?"

"I guess Spencer is white?" I asked hesitantly.

She nodded.

I zoomed out so we could see it normal-sized again and felt the now-familiar tingling at the nape of my neck. I closed my eyes but could still see the image in my mind, except it transformed into someone in a gray hooded sweatshirt peering at me from under the hood. I could hear swearing and smell tea.

"Jane!" My eyes flew open. Jane jumped, startled.

"What is it?"

"I might have seen this person the morning of the robbery."

"What? Where?"

"Right out on Sophia Street. I was sitting on my front steps when you called. The phone startled me and I spilled tea all over the place and was swearing up a storm when I saw him running by. My ranting caused him to break his stride. He glanced over at me, and I waved an apology."

"Wait, you could tell it was a man?"

"Yes," I said excitedly. "It was a man."

"How can we know if it was the same person?"

"We can't without a doubt, but he was wearing a light-colored sweatshirt with the hood up and he was running down Sophia Street. It's gotta be more than a coincidence, right?"

She reflected on it for a second, then asked, "What time did I call you?"

We each scrolled through our recent calls to Monday morning. She got there first. "It was quarter to five," she said.

"Does that fit with the timeline?" I asked excitedly.

"I think so. There's a timestamp." She checked the image. "It was 4:41 when he passed the camera."

"That would work, wouldn't it? It's what, five blocks from here to the church? Could you run it in four minutes?"

"If someone was chasing me." She smiled half-heartedly, but it quickly faded. "Though I bet someone who runs regularly could do it easily. Do you remember anything about him? Was he running like he was running away or just jogging? Could you see his face at all?"

The excitement of the discovery had my heart and mind racing. In an attempt to calm both down, I closed my eyes. I tried to recall the incident clearly, but all I could see was the brief glimpse I'd gotten of him in the midst of cleaning up the mess I'd made. I sighed.

"No, I'm afraid not. I only saw him for a second and the hood was pulled low over his forehead. All I can tell you is he wasn't running as much as jogging, so he didn't seem to be in a hurry."

She was momentarily disappointed, but quickly rallied. "What time is it?" She pressed a button on the side of her phone, and it lit up with the time. "It may be too late to call Gomez, but I can at least text her. She can see if there are other cameras along this end of Sophia Street."

I started to tell her I knew the big houses on the river side of the street had cameras, along with the library, but she was intent on her text, so I waited. Besides, there was some memory about the jogger nagging at me.

"I hope she doesn't wait until Monday to respond," Jane said when she was done. "I want this all to be over with as soon as possible." She slumped into the cushions on the couch.

I couldn't shake the idea I was missing an important clue.

Jane sat up, noting my expression. "What is it? Have you remembered something?"

"No, but there's something bugging me about the jogger, and I can't put my finger on it."

"Did you recognize him?"

"No, that's not it. There was something odd about him." I shook my head as if I could shake loose the memory, but with no success.

It was my turn to slump into the cushions on the couch. "I'm sorry. Whatever was strange about him is not coming to me. It's maddening."

"That's OK. Maybe if we do something else, it will come back to you. That works for me sometimes." She patted my hand.

We finally settled on watching a couple episodes of *Schitt's Creek* rather than a movie because we were too tired to make it through a whole movie, given the time and the wine.

Partway through the first episode Jane got a text from Gomez. She read it out loud. It was short and to the point.

"Excellent. That fits the timeline. We will broaden our search for security cameras in the area," Jane read.

We'd only been watching TV again for a couple minutes when a second text arrived on her phone. I could see it was from Gomez. Jane read the few lines and drew in a sharp breath. She didn't say a word, just handed the phone to me.

We received some of the employment records for Macmillan Jones's store. Mr. Minor worked there for a short while after you let him go.

Jane's eyes were bright with tears. She grabbed the remote and started *Schitt's Creek* to distract herself.

By the middle of the third episode, Jane had fallen asleep sitting up.

I gently nudged her. "I have a bed ready for you upstairs."

Her eyelids fluttered, and she mumbled, "I'll sleep here." She slid down on her side and pulled her legs up on the couch into a fetal position.

I smiled and grabbed the blanket off the couch and laid it over her. I took our wine glasses to the kitchen, put the food away, and put our dinner dishes in the dishwasher. The pots and pans could wait until morning.

On my way to the living room, I grabbed a pillow from the armchair and tucked it under Jane's head. She barely stirred. I picked up her phone from beside her on the couch to put it to the coffee table and dropped it. Luckily, it landed on the carpet and didn't wake her.

As I bent to pick it up, I glimpsed the edge of a brown paper bag between the couch and the end table. It could have been my gift for not seeing things in plain sight, but in my defense, it had been hard to see because it was tucked under the solid oak end table.

"There you are," I whispered.

Jane mumbled and rolled over. I picked up the bag as quietly as possible and carried it with me up to my bedroom, shutting off all the lights except the one under the microwave as I went. I didn't want Jane stumbling on things if she needed to get up during the night.

After I climbed into bed, I carefully pulled the books Sophie had left for Claire out of the bag. They did appear to be quite old. One was *Mademoiselle de Clermont, Nouvelle historique* by Madame Genlis, published in 1811. The title was embossed in gold letters on a standard hardcover. It was frayed a little at the edges but otherwise was in good shape to my average eye. I couldn't read French, but I could get the general idea from the title.

The other book was larger, close to a legal-size piece of paper, and had a thicker, inflexible cover. It felt like there was a hard surface under the leather cover. I found it unusual there was no title on the cover of the book.

I opened it gently and found it was a collection of sheet music. The pages were thick, printed on vellum, and heavier than I expected. There was no publication information except for various dates from the late 1700s and early 1800s on the individual pieces of music.

The same name was gracefully handwritten on a bookplate inside each book. The name was not easy to read in the old-fashioned script, but I knew the first name was Margaret because of what Sophie had told us. The last name definitely began with an M, or was it a V? My eyelids were getting droopy, but I was certain it had to be one of those. M-o or M-a, maybe.

Claire would lecture me for not being able to read cursive well, despite the fact I had learned to write it as a child. It upset her they don't teach children to read and write cursive anymore. Working at a museum, she knew it was essential when trying to read historical documents. Finally, I understood why.

I let my eyes become unfocused on the page and tried to visualize this Margaret with the quill in hand, writing her name all those years ago.

She wasn't writing anymore. Instead, it was me typing my name, only I had written it as Olivia Brown rather than Wilde. I grabbed a pencil and tried to erase it from the screen of my laptop, but it had no effect. In frustration I threw the pencil down and knocked over the cup of tea on the desk. Suddenly, I was on the front stoop with tea all over myself and tears on my cheeks.

Then I heard a sound. I sat still, straining to hear what it was, my inner knowing telling me it was important. There was a rhythmic, muffled thumping sound.

Thump. Thump. Thump.

I saw the jogger running down the street and with each stride there was a muffled thump.

Something touched my arm. I tried to brush it away, but as soon as I made contact with it, I knew it was a hand.

Screaming, I sat bolt upright in bed.

There leaning across the bed, looking as startled as I felt, was a man, who was wearing a dark sweatshirt with the hood pulled up over a ski mask. It was a second before I realized I wasn't still dreaming. He was really there in my bedroom, and he had the books from Sophie in his hands.

I glanced down at them and up at him. He held my eyes for a second but then Jane called my name, and we heard her footsteps moving up the stairs.

He threw the books into a green backpack sitting open on the bed and bolted out of the room. I hadn't even thrown off the covers when I heard Jane scream, followed by the sound of someone falling down.

I ran into the hall and found her scrambling to her feet, She was breathing heavy, clearly terrified.

"Who the hell was that?" she yelled.

I helped steady her. "Are you OK?"

"Yeah, I'm fine."

"Good. Call Gomez." I ran to the stairs. When I looked over my shoulder before descending the steps and saw she hadn't moved yet, I screamed, "Now!"

CHAPTER TWENTY

I leapt down the stairs two at a time and ran to the front door, through which the thief had just disappeared.

I made it out the door in time to catch a glimpse of him rounding the corner of the building to the left as I ran out on the top step of my stoop. Someone called my name, but I ignored it. I flew down the stairs and ran after him. All I could think was I needed to see where he went.

When I rounded the corner, I could see him running down Sophia Street. He had picked up speed and was a half a block ahead of me. I only then realized my feet were bare, but I ran after him anyway.

Glancing over his shoulder, he spotted me following him. He sped up and reached the end of the block before I could close any distance. He vaulted over the guardrail at the end of Sophia, which prevents cars, but apparently not people, from ending up in the yard of the house beyond it. I couldn't imagine where he was planning to go, as there was nothing for blocks but houses on an embankment with steep slopes ending at the river.

When I got to it, I jumped over the guardrail much less athletically than he had, and stopped, catching my breath, and scanning the yard. I couldn't see him, but I heard a sound. I listened intently. It was branches breaking, and it was coming from below me along the river.

As I ran to the edge of the embankment, lights came on behind me in the house in whose yard I was trespassing, followed by a bright spotlight at the roofline that lit up the backyard and the slope down to the river. The light proved helpful because when I leaned over the top of the hill, I could see the track where he had made his way down, slipping and sliding on the muddy soil by the looks of it.

I was debating whether to try to follow him when several things occurred in rapid succession.

First, someone shouted at me from the house. I ignored it because at the same moment, the thief emerged from the cover of the bushes at the bottom of the hill. He was in partial shadow when he looked up at me, but I could see he'd lost his hood and his ski mask during the scramble down the hill. I hadn't registered anything about his face other than it was familiar, when I noticed sirens in the distance.

He must have heard them too. He quickly pulled his hood up and ran off upstream along the riverbank.

"What the hell are you doing in my yard?" came an angry voice from behind me.

I spun around and found a man with a coat on over his pajamas and a flashlight in his hand. I silently offered gratitude it was a flashlight not a gun.

I put my hands up in a gesture of surrender anyway. "I'm so sorry. I live over in Mary Washington Square. There was a burglar in my house, and I followed him down the street."

His eyes went wide.

"I saw him run into your yard and down the hill." We each glanced toward the river.

"Are you all right?" he asked in a gentler tone.

His question made me wonder if Jane was OK, and I turned to the street. The sirens were close now. I knew I needed to talk to the police right away.

"I'm fine. Thank you. I'm sorry if the disturbance scared you and your family. I need to go tell the police what I saw. They'll probably be over here shortly to see if they can find the intruder."

He was not pleased, but nodded and walked back to his house, where I saw a woman watching out the French doors.

I jogged down the street and arrived just as three police cars pulled up. Jane was waiting in the courtyard with Lucia and a small cluster of neighbors.

Jane ran to me as soon as she saw me. "Oh, Liv, thank God." She hugged me tightly. "Are you all right?" She held me at arm's length, checking me over. "Jesus, you're not even wearing shoes."

I shrugged and was going to respond when a police officer interrupted us. The voice was familiar.

"Hello, ladies. Detective Gomez called us regarding a burglar," said Officer Clark.

We spoke over each other. I put my hand on Jane's arm to stop her.

"You have to hurry. I chased him down the street. He went over the guardrail at the end of the block and down the slope and ran upstream along the riverbank."

His eyebrows rose as he took in my appearance—my comfy yoga pants and t-shirt that I sleep in, and my lack of shoes. I was suddenly acutely aware I wasn't wearing a bra, either.

"You chased him?"

"Yes, and he's getting away. I can show you where he went. He left a trail down the embankment."

Officer Clark called over two other officers, telling one to get statements from Jane and the other residents and telling the other to come with him. Clark, the other officer, and I got in one of the police cars and drove the two blocks to the end of the street. He had to let me out of the backseat since it doesn't open from the inside. It was unsettling to know I couldn't let myself out.

The owner of the house was there waiting for us, now fully dressed. Clark told him they would like to inspect his yard for evidence of the suspect, and he showed them to where I'd been standing. I followed and showed the officers the path the thief had made down the hill and pointed out where he'd emerged from the brush before continuing upriver.

Clark reached for his radio, giving instructions for officers to disperse along Caroline Street all the way to Old Mill Park and the Falmouth Bridge and to focus their search along the riverbank.

Looking at me as he said, "The suspect is . . ."

"A white male in a dark, hooded sweatshirt, black jeans and carrying a green backpack."

Clark quickly relayed what I said.

I added, "He had a ski mask with him, but he may have lost it on the way down the hill because he wasn't wearing it when he came out of the bushes."

"Did you see his face?" Officer Clark asked.

"Yes, but just for a second."

Clark spoke with the other officer briefly, gesturing down the hill. We left him there with the homeowner to get a statement from him.

When we arrived at my townhouse complex, we found Detective Gomez standing on the steps from the sidewalk to the courtyard, talking with Jane. It wasn't until I saw Jane standing in the spill from a streetlight, that I noticed some blood at her right temple.

"You're bleeding. Are you all right?" I ran to her side.

Her hand went to her head. "I'm fine." She touched her temple gingerly. "I bumped it on a picture frame on the wall when he knocked me over. It's only a flesh wound," she said with an attempt at humor to deflect my concern.

I huffed out a half-hearted laugh and put my arm around her shoulders.

Officer Clark updated Gomez on the situation. She nodded, apparently approving of what had been done so far.

"Ms. Wilde," she began. "I need you to fill in some details for me." Noting all the neighbors gathered anxiously in the courtyard, she said, "Perhaps we can step inside, so you can warm up and be more comfortable."

It was a clear night, and without clouds to keep any warmth from the day from escaping, it had become chilly.

"OK." I shivered, noticing, now that the adrenaline was wearing off, how cold I was and that the soles of my feet hurt.

Gomez spoke to Clark, who then began to ask the neighbors to return to their homes.

Gomez escorted Jane and me to my door. When we entered, we found Lucia in the kitchen with tea already steeping. I hugged her in thanks and ran upstairs to at least put on a bra.

I felt more presentable when I came downstairs and sat at the counter between the kitchen and living room, Lucia had poured four cups of tea and was offering one to Gomez. I warmed my hands on mine.

Lucia walked around us to the couch and picked up the blanket I had put over Jane only a short while ago. She wrapped it around my shoulders and went upstairs to find another one for Jane, who sat down beside me.

Gomez stood on the other side of the counter in the kitchen facing us and pulled out her ever-present notebook.

"You may have told the story to the other officers, but start from the beginning anyway," she said.

Lucia bustled in with another blanket and put it around Jane. She stood between us with a hand on each of our shoulders.

Gomez looked pointedly at her, and I spoke up.

"Detective Gomez, this is Lucia Leto, my neighbor and friend."

They shook hands, and Lucia remained firmly where she was despite Gomez's stare.

"I'd like her to stay for moral support, if that's all right."

She grimaced slightly but nodded her ascent. She was clearly choosing her battles "So, from the beginning," she said.

Jane and I began telling her everything, but we hadn't gotten far when Jane stopped abruptly, her forehead creasing.

"I think he might have been in the house listening to us."

Gomez and I spoke simultaneously. "What?"

"Why do you say that?" Gomez asked.

Jane addressed her question to me. "Do you remember the noise in the hall? Before you went to lock the door?"

My jaw dropped.

Jane explained to Gomez. "The sound we heard may have been him coming into the house. He must have hidden until we went to bed."

The thought gave me goosebumps all over and I shuddered. Lucia's hand squeezed my shoulder.

"That's so creepy, but it could be possible." I tried to go through my memories of everything that had happened earlier in the night. "I didn't see anything odd when I went to lock the door, but I suppose he could have been in the closet." Then the realization hit me. "Wait, the creak we heard. I recognize it now. It was the hinge on the door of the coat closet. You know the squeak it makes."

Jane's eyes widened in recognition.

"Holy shit!" I said it louder than I intended and made Jane jump.

"What is it?" Gomez asked.

"The backpack on the bed. He had to have been in the closet."

Gomez was looking at me either expectantly or like I had lost it entirely.

"There was a backpack on the bed when I woke up. I presumed he had brought it with him, but—"

Following my train of thought, Jane interrupted. "It was in the closet?"

"Yes. It was one of the girls' old school bags. I thought it seemed familiar, but now I'm certain." I shivered. "So, he really was in the house the whole time."

I pulled the blanket more tightly around my shoulders.

"Did you discuss anything that would have been of importance to him?" Gomez asked, trying to guide the conversation to what was pertinent from her perspective.

Jane spoke first. "Yes. Assuming it was the same person who broke into my store, we talked about him. I showed Liv the still frame you sent me, and she recognized him as the person who'd jogged by the morning of the break-in."

"And then you texted me?" Gomez asked.

"Yes. Then I texted you. So, he must have listened to us talking about all of that. Oh my gosh. That means he heard everything you said, Liv."

"Which was?" Gomez asked.

I tried to describe the feeling I'd had about the jogger, that there was something weird about him I couldn't put my finger on.

Lucia had remained still and silent until this point, but I felt her put slight pressure on the center of my back where her hand rested. I knew what she was encouraging me to do, but I was reluctant to try to tap into my alternate skill set with Jane and Gomez watching me.

"What was weird about him?" Gomez pressed. "Was he unusual physically?"

Heat prickled under my skin. With Lucia's presence behind me, I closed my eyes as much to shut out their stares as to allow the sensation to wash over me rather than fight it. I breathed deeply, calling to mind Angie's instructions during our yoga class meditations. All at once my dream came back to me, and my eyes flew open.

"I had a dream. I was dreaming right before I woke up and saw him. I saw the jogger running by or remembered it or whatever, and there was this rhythmic thumping noise. It wasn't loud, it was kind of muffled, but I could hear it as he ran." I thought suddenly of the grainy photo on Jane's phone. "As if he had something under his sweatshirt!" I shouted triumphantly.

But Gomez expressed only puzzlement.

I addressed Jane, "In the picture it was hard to tell if it was a man or a woman because there was a bump of some kind at the chest, right?" She nodded. "What if he had a way of carrying the books under his sweatshirt, some way to hold them there, but not strapped down tightly, so they bounced a little when he ran? That would explain the thumping."

I caught my breath and plunged on finally getting some clarity on the things that'd been bothering me. "And when I was out walking with Claire and Sophie the other day, we were discussing runners and how they dress, and there was the guy I saw on the way home from the Red Dragon. He was hardly wearing anything at all."

I must have sounded like I was raving. Jane's brow was furrowed with concern.

"Don't you see?" I asked in exasperation. "The man I saw running the morning of the break-in was wearing a heavy sweatshirt with a hood, and sweatpants. If he'd been a real jogger out for a run, he would've been wearing less. He wouldn't have had on such warm clothes because he would've heated up during his run, and then what would he have done with all those clothes? He wasn't out for a jog; he was pretending to be because he was the one who broke into Jane's store."

It might have been a challenge for them to follow the whole line of thought, which was so clear in my mind, but Gomez was able to put enough of it together.

"He pretended to be a jogger out for a run so he wouldn't attract any attention when he ran away from the scene of the crime," she said.

"Yes." I was elated. "That must be it, don't you think? And the sound I couldn't place, was the books he'd stolen hidden under his sweatshirt."

"It's possible," she said, doubtfully.

My mind continued churning and my thoughts and words were a jumble. "Though he must not have known what size the books were going to be. The two I had would've been too big to hide under his sweatshirt without them being obvious. So, he hadn't seen them before."

Pieces were coming together in my mind as fast as more questions were popping up. It was making my head spin.

"But the books I had were never in Jane's store and yet he thought he'd find them there and then here. Unless there were two book thieves, which is unlikely."

Gomez broke into my rambling with her steady voice. "Slow down. Bring us into what you're thinking."

"Sorry. I just realized the books he stole tonight were never in Jane's store. So, if it was the same person, why did he believe they were in the store in the first place and how did he end up here?"

"Those are good questions, which we will ask him ourselves as soon as we have him in custody. For now, let's stick with tonight's events," she said, trying to guide my thoughts. "The priority is finding him. We can work out the details later. You saw him twice tonight, Ms. Wilde. Can you identify him as the person in the image I sent to Ms. Harper? Did you recognize anything at all about him?"

I tried to relax, wiping the sweat from my brow. The surge of energy that had come with the revelations was abating.

Before I had time to ponder her question, Gomez's phone rang. Recognizing the number, she picked it up right away and walked down the hall for privacy.

As soon as Gomez was out of earshot, I asked, "Did you see him? Was it Spencer?"

Jane was taken aback. "I hardly saw him. He burst out of your room and shoved me out of the way as he ran by, and he was wearing a mask."

"What about his height and build? Could they have been similar to Spencer's?"

She considered the question. "I don't know. It happened so fast, and I haven't seen him in so long."

I watched as she tried to pull memories of him up.

"I guess he would have been around the right height. Though I have no idea if his weight has changed since I last saw him." Her hands went up in surrender. "Did you get a look at him?"

"I did for a second, when he came out of the bushes—just a glimpse and he was in the shadows, but his mask had come off." I closed my eyes to try to remember what I'd seen, but soon reopened them, my shoulders sagging. "I can't concentrate."

"Wait, how could we be so stupid?" Jane picked up her phone and tapped quickly away at it for a minute, then held it out to me. "Would a picture of Spencer help?"

She'd done a Google image search on "Spencer Minor" and there were a variety of photos from his social media accounts.

"Is he the person you saw?"

He was an extremely attractive young man with gorgeous green eyes and shaggy brown hair, but he wasn't the man I'd seen. "No. That's not who I saw."

"You're sure?" Jane asked. She sounded relieved.

"Pretty sure," I said. I checked the photos a second time, uncertainty creeping in.

"Hey, why did you ask me earlier if he had a dog?" Jane asked.

I tried to focus on Jane and not on all the thoughts running through my mind. "We thought someone might've been eavesdropping on us at the dog park when you called the other day."

My fingers drummed the counter with nervous energy.

"Wait, after we hung up with you, we talked about the books and what time period they were from, Sophie even started to mention the name that was on the bookplate. It must have been the confirmation he needed. So, it had to be him. He had to be the one listening."

"Who, Spencer?" Jane asked confused.

"No, the thief. Whoever he is." I put my head in my hands. "My thoughts are as jumbled as my words, apparently. I need to concentrate on what I saw."

Lucia moved into the kitchen so she could look at me. She leaned her arms across the counter and took my hands in hers.

"You saw him. It's in your memory somewhere. Be still with it. Don't chase it, let it come to you."

Her voice and her energy were calming. I breathed deeply, trying to let my thoughts become still, which wasn't easy.

She continued, speaking gently, "Was there anything distinctive about his features? Were there any marks you could see on his face or neck, like a mole or a tattoo?"

I began to feel like I was floating, everything became muted but the sound of my own breath in my ears. My mind kept repeating Lucia's words, "Were there any marks you could see?"

I envisioned him peering through the holes in the ski mask from a couple feet away. He definitely didn't have green eyes. I saw again the face quickly covered by the hood in the shadows at the base of the embankment. I knew his face. Were there any marks? Yes, there was one, and suddenly I understood what the last name on the bookplate was, too.

I opened my eyes to find Gomez walking toward us, her lips pressed together, and her brow wrinkled with concern. We all spoke at once.

"What is it?" Jane asked.

"Liv has remembered something." Lucia said.

"I know who it is," I said.

Gomez said, "They found him. They spotted him in Old Mill Park and chased him on foot through the park. He eluded them and made it as far as the Falmouth Bridge. However, there were officers from Stafford on the other end of the bridge by then. They had him cornered."

"Had?" I asked with apprehension creeping up my spine.

"He's sitting on the railing and is threatening to jump." Gomez said grimly.

"But the river is so high," I said, as images of rushing water ran through my mind.

"Yes." Gomez said, her voice taut. "I have to get over there now."

I reached for her arm. I felt her muscles tense, clearly trained to be ready to defend herself, and I quickly let go. "Please. Let me come with you. I know him. I might be able to help."

"You know him?" Jane's voice went up a decibel.

Gomez didn't have time to mess around. "Get some damn shoes and a coat fast and let's go. I'll meet you outside in one minute and you can fill me in on the way."

I ran to my room followed by Jane and Lucia. I grabbed socks and sneakers and threw myself on the floor to put them on while trying to explain. "It was when Lucia said there might be identifying marks. That's when it hit me where I'd seen him before. It's Mark Murray from the museum."

I laced up my shoes and got to my feet.

"Mark? Are you positive?" Jane asked.

"Yes. Now that I realized it, I know it was him I saw at the bottom of the hill.

"But why?" Jane asked.

"I have no idea." I gave her a quick hug. "But call Claire and ask her if she can dig up anything on someone named Margaret Moray in relation to the Monroes. Tell her to spell it m-o-r-a-y and to call me as soon as she finds anything." I grabbed my cell phone and a coat as I ran for the door.

CHAPTER
TWENTY-ONE

G omez was waiting in her unmarked car at the curb, her fingers tapping impatiently on the steering wheel. I climbed in and we sped off down Sophia Street, avoiding the police car parked at the house at the end of the block as we rounded the curve that brought us up to Caroline Street. Gomez switched on the blue police lights but no siren.

As we sped down Caroline toward the bridge, I told her what I knew about Mark, which wasn't much.

"He's the curator at the James Monroe Museum. I know he grew up around here and was married for a short time in his twenties. As far as I know, he doesn't have any kids."

"Do you know if he's had any problems at the museum that would drive him to all of this?"

"No. My friend Claire works there, and I join her for her lunch break occasionally . . ." I trailed off, recalling my last meal at the museum, sitting with Claire under the windows of the building and Ethan telling me he could hear us from inside.

"Shit. I must have tipped him off that the books might not be in Jane's store after all."

"Explain," was all Gomez said.

I filled her in on my last visit to the museum and how Mark must have heard me mention the books I had for Claire.

"If he was listening in on our whole conversation, he knew I was planning to bring them to Claire this Sunday so she could give them to her boss to check out. So, he would have known he needed to get them before Sunday." My mind raced. "He asked me about the break-in and if they had any suspects, and then there was later in day at the dog park." My voice drifted off with my thoughts.

"The dog park?" she prompted.

I realized Gomez hadn't been in the room when I talked to Jane and Lucia about the man at the dog park. I repeated what I'd told them.

"Did you discuss anything other than the security camera footage and the dates and name on the books?" Gomez asked.

I thought about the conversation. "Nothing of significance. You didn't have a lot of information yet. Jane said you were contacting other businesses for footage from other security cameras and—"

"And what?" Gomez prompted again.

I spoke with the excitement of the revelation. "She told us officers were searching in the alleys and along the river for evidence and had found a jacket."

Gomez picked up my train of thought. "And if it was Mr. Murray and he overheard that part, he might have thought he didn't have much time before we could identify him."

She refocused on driving as she made a left on the road next to the VFW and would have taken the next right onto Princess Anne Street, but the street was already clogged with cars in all directions because the police had the bridge blocked off at each end. Flashing lights were everywhere.

My phone rang as Gomez sounded the siren for a moment and pulled her car up on the sidewalk to get as close to the bridge as possible. I dug my phone out of my pocket to see who it was. "It's Claire."

Gomez hesitated. "Quickly find out if she knows anything that can help us get him off the bridge safely." I answered the call as Gomez continued. "But let me be explicit. She is not to speak a word about this to anyone else. No one."

She got out of the car and headed directly for the officers standing at the blockade at the beginning of the bridge.

"Did you hear that, Claire?"

"Loud and clear," she said.

"Good. I guess Jane got hold of you?"

"Yes, she was frantic. Is it true? Is it Mark?"

"I'm afraid so. And if we're going to be able to do anything to help him, we need to do it quickly. Did you find anything on a Margaret Moray?"

"No, but I ran a query on the Papers' database."

The Papers of James Monroe was its own entity, also based at UMW. It was tasked with cataloging all the known papers and correspondence by, to, or related to James Monroe.

"It's not much, but there could be a connection. There was a Margaret Moray who lived here in Fredericksburg and who was a friend of Elizabeth Monroe's. Apparently, they remained friends for the rest of Elizabeth's life. There's one letter in the Papers collection from Margaret to the Monroes' daughter, Maria, offering her condolences after Elizabeth's death. All I could find out through the internet about Margaret was she died here in Fredericksburg three months after Elizabeth did."

I tried to take it all in and one question rose to the surface out of the many running through my mind. "Could there be any connection between the name Moray and Murray?"

I could hear her fingers tapping on a keyboard. *What would we do without the Internet?* I wondered. Claire draw a sharp breath.

"Yes, Murray is the Americanized version of the Scottish name Moray. So, he could be a descendant of Margaret Moray's if the family changed the spelling of their name at some point."

I could see Gomez returning to the car. "Thanks, Claire, I've got to go. Oh, wait—one more thing. Does Mark have a dog?"

"Yes, he does. He has a miniature collie named Mercer. Wha—oh my gosh, you think it was him at the dog park?"

I didn't have time to respond. I ended the call and got out of the car, rushing to meet Gomez.

"What did she say?" she asked, all business as usual. She gestured to the bridge, and I told her what Claire had said as we walked around the barricade.

We stopped there. The scene was like something from a movie. Police cars and fire trucks were everywhere with lights flashing. There was an ambulance too, but I didn't want to consider why it might be needed. Police officers from Fredericksburg and Stafford County were trying to get the last few cars remaining on the bridge out of the way, having them make U-turns, and directing the drivers around the barricades at either end.

The spotlights from several police cars pointed to the center of the bridge, where I could see a figure sitting on the edge of the cement railing. He looked small from where I stood, and my heart went out to him despite what he'd done. I knew the slope of his shoulders wasn't due only to the weight of the backpack. It was a posture I was familiar with, defeated, at your wits' end, lost in grief.

"Is there any way you can let me talk to him?" I asked.

"You said you hardly know him," Gomez said.

"Yes, but he does know me, and there may be a way I can reach him."

"What makes you say that?" she asked, doubtfully.

"I think some kind of grief drove him to this, and that's an emotion I can understand."

The stern line of her mouth softened a little. "Grief? What makes you say that?"

I shrugged. "Call it a sixth sense."

"I'm gonna need more than that."

I looked at Mark. "There's something in his posture I recognize. Please."

I could tell she was trying to decide what to do, and I wanted to say more, but my intuition told me to keep silent.

"He's refused to talk to any officers. He threatens to jump if any of them start to approach him, and once he nearly did. We have a psychologist who works with the department as part of our crisis negotiation team for these kinds of situations, but she's on leave and we're trying to get in touch with her substitute." She was still hesitant. "I might be able to give you some time to see if you can get him to engage in conversation with you, just until we can get the psychologist here to take over."

She paused, as an internal debate raged. "It's best practice for them to talk to someone they aren't acquainted with, but—" Her words trailed off in frustration. There was a hardness in her eyes when she spoke again. "We're trained for this, and you're not. If you do this, you have to be prepared for the idea he might jump no matter what you say or possibly as a result of your presence. These situations are unpredictable."

She went on more gently. "And because of the water level, he would most likely not survive if he jumps. You might have to witness it."

I knew she was being painfully honest on purpose, so I understood the harsh reality of the situation.

"Do you still want to go out there? Can you handle that?"

I took a deep breath, which stuttered on its way out. "Honestly, I'm not sure. But I'd have a harder time living with it if he jumps and I did nothing to try to stop him."

Her internal conflict showed in her body language.

Finally, she said, "OK, you have two minutes to try to get him to start talking."

Two minutes didn't seem like much, which must have been evident in my expression.

"Hopefully, we will have the psychologist here by then."

From my perspective, I could see the long line of unmoving cars over her shoulder. I suspected it would take their psychologist longer than two minutes to get here.

"If he does talk to you, you would need to keep him talking as long as you can, until we can get our person out there. If he makes a move to jump, whatever you do, under no circumstances should you try to physically stop him. He could pull you over with him."

It was a grim warning and the truth of it took my breath away. I was completely terrified, because if I thought he was going to jump, my instinct would be to reach for him. And in my mind, I saw the vision again—I was reaching, and falling, and falling.

CHAPTER TWENTY-TWO

G omez had given me a blanket to offer to Mark and before she let me go told me repeatedly the whole idea was against her better judgment.

I had no clue what I was going to say as I walked slowly to the center of the bridge. I gripped the blanket tightly, like it was some kind of life preserver and hoping somehow that's exactly what it would prove to be. The flashing lights were distracting, but I tried to keep my focus on Mark's small form sitting on the cement railing of the bridge.

He didn't look up at all, fixated on the raging river below.

This might be a different situation if it hadn't been such a rainy month both here and upstream. If the water level was a little lower, it was possible he could survive a jump from this bridge if he landed in the right place, but with the water rushing by the way it was now, the odds were he'd quickly be pulled under and carried away.

I shuddered and shook my head to drive the images of the river out of my mind.

I couldn't tell if he knew someone was approaching or not, but he must have seen movement in his peripheral vision because when I got within around 30 feet of him, he put up a hand and yelled, "I said I didn't want to talk to anyone. Go away or I swear, I'll jump."

I stopped in my tracks. The sound of the water rushing by below was louder out here. I tried to speak loudly enough for him to hear me without shouting.

"Mark, it's me, Liv Wilde." He didn't acknowledge me. "Mark, please, I only want to talk to you. I want to help you."

I thought his eyes might have shifted in my direction. I may have been grasping at straws, but I thought it was a good sign.

"Please. I don't know what you're dealing with, but I do know what loss feels like and how it can eat away at you, make you feel hopeless. But—"

"There is no but," he shouted. "There's no happy ending here. No words of comfort that can make it better. No goddamn support group." His voice trailed off.

My voice was shaky when I spoke, but I wasn't going to give up so soon. "I get it. I really do. I felt the same way after my husband died. How could anyone understand what I was going through? I didn't want to be told about the stages of grief. In fact, there was a point when I wanted to punch anyone who mentioned grief."

Did he turn slightly toward me?

"I admit, I'm no expert. I'm not a psychiatrist. I don't have the right words to say to offer you comfort. But I care about you, and there are many others who do, too. And I'm willing to listen, to just be here with you in case you want to tell me what this is all about."

He didn't tell me to go to hell, so I took one step forward. As quietly as I could, while still allowing him to hear me, I said, "Does it have anything to do with Margaret Moray? Is she an ancestor of yours?"

He finally turned his head and shoulders a bit and nodded.

It terrified me to see his body move on the railing at all. The Falmouth Bridge was notorious for its crumbling cement railings and occasional potholes so deep they gave a glimpse of the river below. I tried to hold his eyes and not look at the river or the railing.

"She lived hundreds of years ago. What does she have to do with all this?"

"Hundreds of years ago." He practically spat the words out. "You don't understand a thing," he said disdainfully, his attention on the water again. "Go away."

I was terrified I'd said the wrong thing and that his agitation would cause him to jump or lose his balance and fall. My heart was pounding in my chest, and I could barely breathe. I was scared I was close to pushing him over the edge myself with my words.

Suddenly, I heard Lucia telling me to trust my intuition. So, I told my brain to shut the hell up and put my hand on my heart.

"You're right, I don't understand. I have no idea what you're going through, and I won't lie and tell you I do. I hate it when people do that. All I can tell you is when I look at you, I see grief and that's a subject I know a little about. So, tell me, what is it you're grieving?"

It was as if everything around us went silent. There was only me and Mark. He hung his head, and I saw him wipe away tears.

I spoke gently. "Mark, can I at least bring you this blanket? You must be cold."

He nodded, but as soon as I took my first step there was activity on the bridge behind us. The officers had moved closer when I did.

He glanced to the left and right and screamed, "Tell them to stay away!" The franticness in his voice scared me.

I held up my hands to the officers and mouthed "please" over my shoulder to Gomez, hoping she could read lips.

She signaled for the officers to retreat a few steps but gave me a warning stare.

"They've stepped back. It's just me. If it's OK, I will come over there and leave the blanket on the railing next to you. Would that be all right?" I asked.

He nodded, watching me as I slowly approached.

I held out the blanket so he could see it and placed it on the railing a foot away from him, so he could pick it up without having to reach for it. I took a couple steps backwards and stopped there.

He reached for the blanket.

"Carefully," I said.

He almost smiled then and slowly wrapped it around his shoulders on top of the backpack, which was still strapped on over his sweatshirt.

I leaned against the railing a few feet away from him, still trying to ignore the water below. "What is it you've lost?"

"What haven't I lost? Pride, dignity, the ability to hold my head up in this damn town. Hope." If possible, he sounded even more sad. "Or maybe the truth is I never had any of them to begin with. That I didn't stand a chance from the day I was born."

He raised his eyes up from the river, his gaze now fixed in the direction of downtown. He sighed heavily.

Without knowing his family or childhood, I wasn't certain why he felt the way he did. So, I asked quietly, "Why would that be? Why from the day you were born?"

He kind of laughed, while shaking his head. "I'm shocked you don't already know about my family. You've lived here long enough to have been told the stories by now. Surely Claire has mentioned it." He glanced at me as if to gauge my reaction.

"I haven't heard any stories about your family. It might not be as bad as it seems."

I'd said the wrong thing again.

"Not as bad as it seems?" The pitch of his voice rose. "Not as bad as it seems? Perfect. I'm blowing it out of proportion, I suppose. Go away, Liv."

I tried to make up for my mistake. "I'm sorry. You're right. You're absolutely right. It was a stupid thing to say." I held up my hands. "This may be the wrong thing to say too, but I don't have a lot of experience with talking to people who are threatening to throw themselves off bridges." I took a deep, unsteady breath. "In fact, I'm notorious for saying the wrong thing at the wrong time. So, I'm bound to say the wrong things now, especially in this extremely stressful situation, but all I want is to let you know I genuinely care."

I let the words hang there between us, hoping he would sense I meant them.

When he didn't tell me to go away again, I asked, "I know you're related to someone who was friends with Elizabeth Monroe and since that sounds like a good thing to me, there must be something else I'm missing. So, what is it about your family I don't know?"

"Yes, it would have been so nice if Margaret's story had been the one that stuck, the one people still remember today. That's why I was doing all this in the first place."

He gestured over his shoulder with his chin, and it finally registered in my brain he had the books there in the backpack, so, if he jumped, they would also be lost, along with whatever importance they held.

I was afraid of saying the wrong thing again, so I remained silent.

"But no, this place has a much longer memory for traitors." I couldn't tell if he was talking to himself or to me. "All I wanted to do was change the story of my family, even if the family line ended with me." He looked down at the water and I froze. "But it can end with me right now."

"No!" I shouted as he swayed forward. "Please, don't." My voice broke with emotion and pleading.

He didn't acknowledge me, but he didn't jump, either. Suddenly, I understood what people meant when they said they could feel their heart in their throat.

"Please. I actually do understand family legacies that are not what we want them to be." I rushed to add, "Not like yours, maybe, but I recently found out something about my grandmother that I never knew. It was a secret in my family because my grandfather forbade my mother to mention it. Yet, I found out anyway." I felt tears rising. "So, I understand how family history has a way of haunting its descendants."

He appeared to be listening intently, and I continued, "Like you said, your family has a story. Maybe there's a way for you to tell it that can change the narrative. A way for you to reclaim and redefine the story."

His head tilted, as if to hear me better.

"It's your story now, Mark, and you're a historian. As hard as it might be to see at the moment, you could be the perfect person in your family tree to tell your family's history and maybe even to embrace it."

"Who would embrace a traitor?" he asked.

I didn't want to press him, but I felt like we were making progress, so I asked tentatively, "A traitor to what?"

He waved an arm in the air toward the town and the surrounding area. "A traitor to the grand old Confederacy, of course. What else would matter around here?" He tucked his arm back under the blanket. It bothered me he wasn't holding on to the railing, but I said nothing. "My great, great, great, great Aunt Betty Murray. They never proved she did anything wrong, mind you, but it didn't matter. She sympathized with slaves. She hired former slaves, which was as good as being an abolitionist. And when they discovered her employee had been sending messages across the river to the damn Yankees, well, that's a legacy you can't walk away from in the South."

I was amazed I'd never heard the story and that it was still impacting his family.

"And people still hold it against your family? Even now?"

He huffed, as if I was unbelievably stupid. "Even now? You say it like it's unimaginable. You've seen the news over the past few years. You know what happened in Charlottesville. You've seen the Confederate flags. Of course, it still matters. They might not say it to my face now, but they did when my father was a boy. They bullied him his entire childhood. They shunned his family. He almost didn't finish high school because he couldn't stand the constant bullying. It was a little different for me since the schools were integrated by then and so the good ol' boy talk about the Lost Cause had gotten quieter. But he had to struggle to make a decent life for me and Mom even generations later."

His voice cracked. "He wanted to start his own business. He was a talented carpenter, but who would have gone to Murray and Son? No one." There was venom in his words. "So, he worked for someone else his whole life, barely scraping by. He was determined I'd get out of this place and make a different life. He cried when he apologized to me before he died."

Tears fell down his cheeks. "I was thirteen when they found the cancer. He'd been trying to save for me to go to college, but he knew the hospital bills would take most of what he'd put aside. Eventually, he refused treatment, hoping to save some money for us. Fancy cancer treatments are only for rich people with good insurance."

I took a step closer. More than anything, I wanted to hug him, but I didn't want to startle him.

"You did manage to go to college, though," I said quietly. "I'm sorry he didn't get to see it."

"I didn't manage it with any help from the people around here," he said with evident bitterness. "Lots of other kids with worse grades than me, got scholarships from churches and civic organizations, but those kids had connections, those kids had family names people didn't whisper about. So, I worked my way through college. I couldn't escape history, so I studied it instead. I thought I could–" He shook his head. "I don't know what I thought I could do."

He looked up at the sky and shrugged.

"I never should've come home. I should've known better. I told myself that having been away I could put it all behind me. I could return and raise up our family name somehow."

"Didn't you, though? You got a good job at the museum. You were doing well there, weren't you? The staff think very highly of you," I offered.

"There were too many ghosts," he said. "Too many memories." He was temporarily lost in his own reflections. "I was planning to leave. I was going to find a job somewhere else and put it all behind me."

"What made you stay?"

"My Aunt Mabel died. That's what made me stay." He sighed. "It always comes down to family. You try to leave, and they find a way to pull you back."

"How did your aunt do that?" I asked.

I could see behind him several police officers had moved slowly closer while he was distracted by our conversation. I assumed the officers behind me were doing the same, but I prayed he wouldn't notice if I could keep him talking.

"She was a pack rat, the hoarder in the family. She left my mom boxes of old family letters, a few books, and photos that had been handed down through the generations. Mom thought I might enjoy going through them. She thought there might finally be someone in the family who'd find them interesting." He let out something between a sigh and a scream. "If only I'd left and never opened those boxes. But I went through them. I couldn't help it."

He stared down at his hands as if he were holding an object in them. "And I found a letter. For a short time, it gave me hope like I hadn't felt in an awfully long time. A way out for my mom and me. It was a letter written so long ago it was on parchment."

He smiled, as if the historian in him still couldn't help but be excited by the thought. "It was written by Margaret Moray, friend of Elizabeth Monroe. She'd contracted yellow fever three months after Elizabeth died, and within days was on her own deathbed. Some of it was difficult to decipher. Her hand must have been shaking with her illness, but she needed to tell someone her secret."

He gazed into the distance as if he could see the scene. "It was a note to her daughter, Mae, telling her there were letters written by James and Elizabeth Monroe hidden in a music book Elizabeth had left to her, letters she'd entrusted to her before she died. Elizabeth had wanted them to remain hidden until an appointed time. The note had probably been set aside by a servant and forgotten when Margaret died so suddenly. Somehow it ended up between the pages of a family Bible I found at the bottom of a box of my aunt's things."

"So, the music book Sophie gave me from the library might be Elizabeth Monroe's, with the letters hidden inside?" I found the story enthralled me.

"There's a good possibility it is. The woman who donated them was a neighbor of my aunt's. But I didn't have time to check inside it. Did you?" There was a touch of eagerness in his tone, which I took as another positive sign.

"Yes, and it did have Margaret's name inside."

His eyes brightened.

"I didn't see Elizabeth's name, though."

We were both quiet until I gently broke the silence. "We could look at the book together and see if we can find the letters."

His voice held so much sadness. "They won't let me do that. They're going to throw me in jail. I did all of this for nothing. All I did was bring more shame on my family."

He gazed almost longingly down at the rushing water.

Things had taken a wrong turn again, but I made one last effort to convince him.

"But it's not for nothing. If those letters are in there, you have an incredible opportunity to change your family's fortunes."

He shook his head. "The letters won't belong to me. I won't be able to sell them."

"It doesn't matter who owns them. They are part of your family history, and only you can tell the complete story of who Elizabeth gave them to." A sense of clarity came over me and my temperature began to rise as if on cue, despite the cold. I spoke the words, yet it felt like they were coming from somewhere else. "You can tell your *whole* family history, rather than letting just one part of it be known. You can write it."

My voice rose with excitement. "You get to control the narrative this time. After all, to some your aunt was a traitor in the Civil War, but to many others she would be a heroine. You can rewrite the story and give her the credit she deserves. Your family has done amazing things, Mark."

The slump of his shoulders remained the same, and I wondered if my words were reaching him.

"Imagine the story you can tell if those letters become part of the historical record."

He smiled and I was hopeful he could finally see a way out of the mess he felt trapped in.

"Maybe," he said slowly. "But I won't be able to see the letters from jail."

He waved a hand in the direction of the police officers who had continued to get gradually closer and were now just twenty feet away.

"I know the detective in charge of the case. She'll listen to you, and if Jane isn't willing to press charges and neither am I—" I let the words sink in. "Come on. Let's get off this bridge. It's getting cold."

His eyes were a mixture of tears and fear and perhaps a glimmer of the hope he'd lost. He nodded ever so slightly and twisted his body to put his right foot down on the outside edge of the railing.

I watched in horror as the cement under his foot gave way.

People say in a life-threatening situation everything happens in slow motion, while contradictorily, you don't have time to think, only to react. Now, I knew it was true, and it was a good thing because if I'd had a minute to consider what I was doing, I might not have made the same choice.

As soon as he felt the cement give way, Mark eyes filled with panic. He grabbed for the railing. Maybe his hands were cold from sitting there so long or maybe he couldn't get a grip on the hard surface, but his hands scraped across the top of the railing without being able to hold on to it.

I felt nothing but dread as I saw him begin to fall away from the railing while I ran the two steps to where he was. People were yelling and there was movement behind me, but I didn't know what they were saying or doing.

I did the only thing I could do. I leaned out across the railing and grabbed hold of his arms. His backward momentum had begun to take over and I found myself moving with him.

I saw my dread reflected in his eyes.

With resignation he said, "Let go, Liv."

I ignored his words and pulled with every ounce of strength I could muster, but still felt my feet lifting off the ground beneath me. I watched with terror as the blanket slipped from his shoulders and floated down to the water below. It was quickly swept up by the current and disappeared under the churning water within seconds.

"No!" I screamed, trying to make my feet stay on the ground with the force of my will alone.

There were other cries in addition to mine.

A strange calm came over me when it registered somewhere in my brain that we were going to fall, that I was going to go over the railing and plummet into the water below where I would probably drown, if I wasn't killed by landing on rocks first. I thought fleetingly of Nate and seeing him again, but then I saw images of my daughters and tears ran down my face.

I held on tighter to Mark's arms as his other foot finally lost its battle with the railing and he began to fall. Trying to hold his full weight caused my feet to lift completely off the cement surface of the bridge.

I felt arms go around my waist, holding me so tightly I could hardly breathe.

"Hold on," someone whispered in my ear.

I didn't know if they meant for me to hang on or to hold on to Mark, but I kept hold of him even as his feet were dangling freely below him. I thought my arms would come out of their sockets. I could feel the cement of the railing bruising my arms as the person holding me leaned back using their weight like an anchor.

Suddenly there was movement all around me. Several people grabbed hold of me keeping me in place while several more leaned over the railing grabbing hold of Mark whose eyes were wild with terror. Slowly they were able to pull him up to the railing where he could get his feet under him.

I was still holding his arms and wouldn't let anyone pry them loose until after I saw officers help Mark swing one leg safely over the railing. Only then did I release his arms, which were swiftly wrenched behind him and placed in handcuffs.

I reached out to him, saying, "No. Don't."

Someone was keeping me from moving after him as they took him away.

"Wait, goddamn it!" I yelled.

They stopped and Mark turned toward me. He looked wrecked. "It's OK," he said and offered a weak smile. "Thank you."

I squinted into the flashing lights as they escorted him to one of the City of Fredericksburg police cars.

Whoever had been holding on to me finally let go and I spun in a fury to confront them.

Detective Gomez met me with a fury of her own. "What was the one goddamn thing I told you not to do under any circumstances?" she yelled.

That's when the edges of my vision started to go black.

CHAPTER
TWENTY-THREE

I awoke to sunlight streaming in through an unfamiliar window and sounds I didn't recognize. I sat up abruptly, realizing I was in a hospital room. Bailey was asleep in a chair but stirred as Jane entered the room with a cup of coffee in each hand.

"You're awake," Jane exclaimed.

Bailey was instantly fully awake. She leapt out of the chair and ran to my side, taking my hand in hers, cheeks wet with tears.

"Mom." She leaned over and her arms went around me in a hug I wanted to last forever.

As I held her, sharp pain shot through my shoulders, but I knew it was nothing compared to the pain she was feeling.

"Oh, baby, I'm so sorry I scared you."

She was sobbing on my shoulder. Jane had put the coffee cups down and was gently rubbing Bailey's back.

After her tears subsided, she stood up and her hands went immediately to her hips. It was like seeing myself in a mirror.

"How could you be so reckless?" Her voice was dangerously close to a scream. "What were you thinking? What would Izzy and I have done without you?" She barely got the last word out before breaking down in sobs again and throwing herself into my waiting arms. "We're so mad at you, Mom," she sobbed.

The raised voices had brought a nurse to the door, but she waited there patiently as we cried and held one another.

"I'm so sorry, baby. I'm so sorry," I said over and over as I held her and stroked her hair, which was curly and brown like Nate's. "I'm right here. I'm not going anywhere." I rocked her in my arms until her fear, grief, and tears abated, at least temporarily.

She sat on the edge of the bed beside me, and I wiped away her tears.

Jane picked up a box of tissues on the tray table beside the bed and offered it to Bailey, who took one and blew her nose loudly.

"Got all the yelling out of your system?" said the nurse, striding into the room and smiling at Bailey.

I winced as I reached up to rub Bailey's arm. "Where's Izzy?" I asked.

"She's at home with Sophie," Bailey answered with a sniff. "Sophie stayed with her there last night. They wouldn't let us both stay here overnight." She gave the nurse a withering glare, which she ignored.

A fresh flood of tears rolled down my cheeks. "I'm so sorry, B."

"That's enough of that for now. You're going to live quite a few more years, I imagine," the nurse said as she moved around the bed to check my vital signs.

I smiled at Bailey and suggested she go call her sister to let her know I was awake while the nurse went through her routine.

She went into the hall with the phone already to her ear. I heard her say, "She's awake," as she walked away.

The nurse went about her business efficiently, but I interrupted her with a question. "When can I leave?"

She pretended to be offended. "You don't enjoy my company?" she asked, then shushed me while she tapped a couple times on an electronic tablet she carried with her. "Don't you even want to know how the surgery went?" she asked.

My mouth fell open.

Her face broke into a smile. "I wanted to see if you were really awake," she laughed.

I raised my eyebrows at Jane, who laughed with her.

"The doctor should be in within the next half-hour. She will determine whether it's time for you to go home. You did a good job on those shoulders based on the results from the ultrasound, but luckily there was no significant damage. The doctor will fill you in when she comes in. From what I've been told, you're lucky your shoulders didn't get dislocated."

She read the display linked to the blood pressure cuff that had been squeezing my arm painfully tight a moment ago and entered more data on her tablet. "If the story's true, you're either a hero or a lunatic."

"Lunatic," responded two people simultaneously.

One was Jane and looking in the direction of the other voice, I saw Detective Gomez leaning against the doorframe. She smiled at Jane as she entered the room and came to stand next to the bed.

Gomez nodded at the nurse, who said to me. "I will tell Doctor Costa you're awake."

I waited until she closed the door behind her before asking Gomez, "How's Mark? Is he all right? Did you let him go? Did he find the letters?"

She didn't have a chance to say anything as the questions spilled out of me. When I paused for breath, she asked, "Are you done?"

I smiled, and she continued. "Mr. Murray is in police custody."

I started to object, but she talked over me.

"He has several things to answer for and since you were unavailable for consultation," she looked at me sternly. "We held him overnight pending charges."

"What about the books and the letters?" I asked more calmly.

"The books are in the custody of the Fredericksburg Police Department."

I opened my mouth again, but this time Jane stopped me.

"Would you let her finish," she admonished.

Gomez wore the patient expression you would use for an unruly child.

I crossed my arms over my chest, making me wince. I was beginning to understand I might have done some real damage to my shoulders. I let them rest at my sides.

Gomez was more sympathetic after that. "The books have not yet been examined for any hidden letters. We were unwilling to do it ourselves for fear of risking damage to what apparently might be historically significant documents. So, we've arranged for two experts to assess the books this afternoon at the police station, since they're evidence in a crime."

She checked the clock on the wall, which read 8:45. "Which will happen in a just over three hours."

"High noon?" I asked.

Her lips twitched, but she ignored my question. "If the good doctor releases you in time"—I sat up excitedly, and she raised her hand—"and if you promise to abide by my instructions for a change, you and Ms. Harper will be allowed to be there as witnesses."

Despite her admonishment, she was smiling broadly now, and I found myself doing the same. She moved as if to leave, but I reached out for her arm to stop her.

I thought of the arms holding me in place on the bridge last night. "Detective, you saved my life last night, didn't you?" I found tears rising in my eyes once more.

She merely nodded. "Let's hope I'll never have to do it again."

"Thank you," I said, my voice choked with emotion.

She touched my hand, still resting on her arm, said goodbye to Jane and left the room.

It was a bit of a struggle to get myself dressed after the doctor gave me my release paperwork two hours later, but Bailey and Izzy were there to help.

Doctor Costa said I'd have some pain in my shoulders for weeks due to muscle strains and tiny tears in the rotator cuffs, but that with rest and physical therapy they should heal completely with no long-term issues. Based on my pain level, she said ibuprofen taken up to three times a day should do the trick, told me to schedule a follow-up visit with an orthopedic doctor, and wished me a good day.

She had no idea just how good of a day I was hoping it would be.

CHAPTER TWENTY-FOUR

I had enough time to go home, get a brief lecture and several big hugs from Izzy, take a quick, moderately painful shower, and make a sandwich to take in the car with me. I found I was starving.

The girls and I agreed we would have a big feast and movie night when I got back, and I left with Jane for the police station.

Gomez hadn't said which two experts would inspect the books. However, when she ushered us into one of the rooms we'd passed on our way to her office a few days before, I wasn't surprised to find Ethan waiting. It was natural they would've contacted one of the local people with the most knowledge of the Monroes.

As we waited for whoever else would be arriving and I took in the room, a memory stirred. The walls were a plain, pale gray. There was one panel of fluorescent lights. There was nothing in the way of furniture except the metal table in the center of the room which had bolts at the base of the legs attaching it to the floor, and a few uncomfortable chairs.

Nothing a person could use as a weapon.

The top of the table was covered in plastic and a desk lamp was shedding a bright light on the center of the table. It was the plastic on the table that triggered the memory. The room was exactly the same as the one I'd seen a flash of in my mind when Gomez had followed up with Jane at the store. The one difference was that on top of the plastic on the table were several pairs of cloth gloves and the two books I'd been inspecting the previous night.

Could it truly have been just last night?

I began to step nearer to the table to study the books more closely, when the door opened behind me.

I expected to see someone from the staff of the Papers of James Monroe entering the room, but instead was delighted to see Mark escorted in by Officer Clark and the female officer I'd seen at Jane's store the day of the break-in. I was happy to see Mark wasn't in handcuffs but was concerned by how pale he was. His demeanor, tousled hair, and rumpled clothes said he'd had better nights, but he smiled when he saw me.

There was a pause when he neared Ethan. I didn't have any idea how much of the story he'd been told.

Mark met Ethan's gaze. "I'm so sorry, Ethan."

They held each other's eyes briefly, but quickly shifted their attention to the books on the table. Their faces were lit with anticipation.

Ethan said with barely suppressed glee, "Let's see what we can find."

Mark walked eagerly over to stand beside Ethan and they each picked up a pair of gloves. It was a bit cozy with all of us in the small room, but Jane, Gomez, Officer Clark, the other officer, and I all remained still and silent, not wanting to miss a thing.

From then on, it was as if everything else fell away for the two men examining the books. They were as excited as children on Christmas morning.

They made a cursory inspection of Madame Genlis's novel, flipping gently through its pages, but it was the music book that called to them. As I had seen last night, the music book wasn't the kind of book with hundreds of pages that could have a space cut out in the middle for hiding valuables. So, I had no idea where they thought they might discover the letters.

It was odd to see two grown men handle a book with such tenderness. Ethan even let Mark do the honors of opening the music book. They both inspected the bookplate on which Margaret Moray had written her name. They checked inside the back cover too, hoping to find some sign it had belonged to Elizabeth Monroe. Their excitement ebbed when they found nothing, but they quickly refocused on the front cover.

They tapped gently on the leather as if hoping to discover a hollow space underneath. Their brows creased at the resulting dull thud instead.

Ethan pulled a small, brown leather case out of his pocket. Opening it, he withdrew a pair of tweezers. He began to carefully lift the edges of the thick paper covering the wood on the inside of the cover. It was a painstaking process to remove the paper without tearing it, but once they had lifted it enough to peer underneath their eagerness transformed to disappointment. Ethan pulled the paper a little further still, to reveal nothing but the board.

As he laid the paper in place, trying to press the corners down until he could properly adhere them again, I saw Mark's attention drawn to the upper corner where the bookplate was. He put his hand on Ethan's wrist and asked him for the tweezers.

Lifting the paper inside the cover had caused a corner of the bookplate to come free. From his angle, Mark must have seen something underneath it. Using the tweezers, he lifted the corner of the bookplate with glacial slowness.

Ethan watched intently, and we all found ourselves unconsciously leaning closer to the table. Mark pulled the bookplate free and there beneath it was another, similar bookplate on which was written in an elegant, feminine hand, *Elizabeth Kortright Monroe.*

Mark and Ethan let out gasps of delight and began to talk over one another.

"It really was hers," said Mark. There was a note of incredulity in his voice, and I realized he must have harbored a modicum of doubt about whether the story in the letter had been true.

"What a find." Ethan said at the same time. His eyes were absolutely dancing with joy.

"It confirms it was her book, but where are the letters?" Mark asked.

Ethan's joy dimmed, but he quickly perked up. "Let's try the back cover."

They went through the same process and to the dismay of all watching, found no hidden compartment or letters there either. They stood looking at the book as if its secrets would be revealed if they stared at it long enough.

"Still, even without the letters, it's an important find, isn't it?" Jane asked.

Ethan seemed startled to find us all standing there watching so attentively. He recovered himself. "Yes. Yes, it is. We have a music book in the collection at the museum, but it is their daughter Maria's. This will give us a basis for comparison—"

Whatever he said next faded away as I felt the heat rise in my body. I was too tired to tell if it was caused by the exhaustion I was experiencing, a hot flash, or an emerging vision.

Gomez must have seen me sway. She pulled a chair over and motioned for me to sit. I took the seat thankfully and closed my eyes, taking a few deep breaths. I felt the tell-tale prickly sensation at the nape of my neck and opened my eyes.

Ethan was still expounding on the possible information about the time period they could discern by studying Elizabeth's music book, but Mark continued examining at the book. I watched as he cautiously flipped through the pages. From my new vantage point, I found the desk lamp blocked my view, so

I reached out and slid it to the left. Mark grinned down at me, and I felt silly for moving the lamp for my own convenience.

Mark started to flip another page, holding it momentarily perpendicular to the binding.

I gasped. The room went quiet, and I whispered into the silence, "Stop. Keep the page straight up vertically."

He did as I asked.

Because I'd moved the light, from my angle in the chair it now shone from behind the book, illuminating the page in his hand. I leaned closer and motioned for Ethan to get down beside me.

He kneeled at my side, and I said, "Can you see words between the lines of the music? Behind them?"

I said it so quietly I wasn't sure he could even hear me, but he leaned closer to the book, bending down further to get a different angle. Though the paper was thick, with the light shining directly through it, something else had become visible. He let out a sound of astonishment.

"Yes, I can." His voice was hushed. "It's faint, but it's there. Mark, do you see it?"

He reached up from where he knelt and held the page in his gloved hand so Mark could reposition himself.

"Oh my God." Mark's expression was one of wonder. "The sunlight," he said.

Everyone was holding their breath.

Ethan broke the delicate silence. "The sunlight?"

Mark beamed. "Yes, in the letter Margaret wrote, she said she sat in the sunlight when she checked to see if Eliza's secret was still safe. It never occurred to me she actually needed the light to see the letters."

Both men hurried to their previous positions at the table, scrutinizing the edges of the pages.

Mark eagerly scanned the room for Gomez. When he found her, he said, "Do you have some kind of magnifier around here?"

She spoke to the female officer, who ran out and returned within seconds with what looked like a short desk lamp, but which was a lighted magnifier on a stand. The officer handed it to Ethan, who plugged it in.

He waved me closer. "Can you hold this up over the table for us?" he asked as he switched the magnifier's light on.

I stood, now energized with excitement, and took it from his hand, holding it in the air above the table while they both inspected the sheet music from the opposite side with the light streaming through.

"There are definitely words there," Ethan said excitedly.

Then Ethan did something making him forever a prince in my mind. He picked up the tweezers and extended his hand to Mark.

"It was your ancestor who was entrusted with these letters."

Someone had filled Ethan in on Mark's family history.

At first, I wasn't sure if Mark would take them or if he was even breathing. But Ethan broke the spell by nodding at the tweezers, and Mark took them from his hand.

They gave me instructions for positioning the light in a way that allowed them to see through it to the pages below. It required some maneuvering to get it to where it would help them without getting the heat too close to the paper. Once we got it there, my job was to stand as still as possible while they worked. It eventually made my arms ache, but the thrill of what we might find overrode the discomfort.

Ethan held the page steady while Mark worked with the tweezers at the edge of one corner of the page, trying to see if there was anything to pry apart. He asked me to make minor adjustments with the light as he went along.

Standing so close, I was able to watch what he was doing through the magnifier. With incredible patience he was able to get one tip of the tweezers in between the two sheets of music, which had apparently been glued together. It would've been impossible to see the seam without the magnifier.

Slowly and gently, so as not to tear the sheet music, he was able to move the tweezers millimeter by millimeter along the page separating the two pieces of paper.

No one spoke or made a sound.

When Mark finally got to the opposite corner with the tweezers, Ethan gently laid the pages down flat. He used the tip of a pencil from his pocket to create a gap and hold them slightly apart while Mark put his cheek down on the table to peer into the gap.

He looked up at Ethan with awe. "It looks like there's a piece of paper in there."

"Can you reach it with the tweezers?" Ethan asked breathlessly.

With a steadier hand than I would've believed possible, Mark slid the tweezers inside. It took him three tries, but gradually and with great care he was able to ease out a thin sheet of parchment. He laid it flat on the plastic and he and Ethan leaned over it.

At the top of the browned surface of the parchment was written in script, "My dear Eliza," and at the bottom it was signed, "Believe me my dear Eliza most affectionately yours, Jas Monroe." The rest of the content was, to my eye, mostly illegible, but Ethan and Mark were taking in every word, from time to time pointing to a word and figuring it out together.

There were tears on both men's cheeks.

Over the course of the next two hours, we took turns holding the magnifier for them as they pried pages apart, which allowed everyone a chance to be part of the discovery when a new letter emerged. In total, they extracted ten letters hidden between the sheets of music. Eight of them written by James to Elizabeth, and two by Elizabeth to James. Mark explained that Margaret's letter indicated the letters from Elizabeth were drafts of letters she'd subsequently rewritten and sent to James.

Ethan and Mark agreed the letters were a find of great historical significance, and no one in the room was unmoved by witnessing their discovery.

CHAPTER
TWENTY-FIVE

A fter four months, enough time had been spent poring
over the letters, enough preliminary research had been
done, and enough hype had been generated that the museum
was ready to reveal them to the world in a big press conference
on the UMW campus.

With the help of an appropriately chastised Sophie, Ethan
had been able to establish the provenance of the books be-
queathed to the library. The donor had been Agnes Holt, an
elderly neighbor of Mark's Aunt Mabel. Neither woman had
been aware of the treasures one of the books held.

Since it could not be established definitively whether the
books had been given to or only loaned to Mrs. Holt, the ownership fell to the local library system, which was funded through
the surrounding counties and the City of Fredericksburg. A
great deal of maneuvering had to be undertaken by the Commonwealth's attorneys to avoid an ugly, sprawling lawsuit over
the ownership of the books. In the end, because of the incredible

historic value of the letters and the accompanying prestige, the Board of Regents for the museum and the Board of Visitors from UMW were able to persuade the legislature to approve a sizable emergency allocation of funds, which when added to a substantial donation from an anonymous UMW alumnus, was given to the library system in compensation for the books. The Commonwealth's attorneys had subtly pointed out that technically a library employee had donated the books to the museum and since whatever compensation they received would save the localities who funded the library's budget the equivalent amount in their own budgets, they acquiesced somewhat willingly.

The museum board thought it only right to list the books as acquisitions courtesy of the Holt and Murray families of Fredericksburg and the Central Rappahannock Regional Library.

As soon as the ownership had been satisfactorily established in the museum's name, the planning for an announcement regarding the books and the letters had begun in earnest.

I arrived at the entrance of the ballroom in the University Center on the day of the press conference to find the room packed with historians and press from all over the world. The room was abuzz with excited conversations.

I spotted Claire involved in an animated conversation with her fellow guides from the museum and saw Ethan at the front of the room talking with the president of the university.

There weren't many empty seats in the front, but there were several in the last couple rows. I chose one and settled myself in. Soon after, I felt someone sit next to me.

I turned to find Mark smiling at me. We shared an awkward hug from our seated positions. He was thin but looked better than the last time I'd seen him.

Jane and I had declined to press charges. However, due to the large police and emergency presence his actions had prompted on the bridge, the judge had sentenced him to a year in the Rappahannock Regional Jail. Because of his guilty plea, cooperation with the police, and it being a first offense, the judge waived the remaining nine months of his sentence for the time already served while awaiting his court date. In addition, he'd had to pay a sizable fine and had been required to undergo mental health counseling.

"It's quite a crowd," I said.

"Yes, the news spread quickly among historians, particularly those who study the Early Republic," he said.

We took in the scene. The air in the room felt electrified.

"What's next for you?" I asked. "Will you be able to return to the museum?"

He shook his head. While he seemed sad, I sensed another emotion under the surface.

"No. Ethan was exceedingly kind about the whole thing. He was willing to go to bat for me with the Board. He thought we could arrange a leave of absence and once things settled down, I could come back." He studied his hands before continuing.

"But as kind as the offer was, I didn't want to put him through the hassle it would require."

"So, what will you do? Will you take some time off?"

He beamed at me. "I'm going to take your advice."

"My advice?"

"Yeah, I talked it over with my mom and my dad's brother, and I'm going to rewrite our family's history. I'm going to write a book about the infamous Murrays."

I was happy to note almost all the bitterness was gone from his voice when he spoke of his family. It had been replaced by anticipation. I gestured toward the introductory slide projected on a screen at the back of the stage which read "The Monroe Letters" followed by a list of the donors' names.

"Don't you mean the *famous* Murrays?" We both smiled and I added, "I read books for a living, so I'm picky about what books I choose for myself, and that's one I would love to read."

His smile faded and his voice was deep with emotion when he spoke. "Thank you."

I opened my mouth to deflect the words, but he spoke over me.

"Seriously." He paused until I met his gaze. "You saved my life. And you gave my family a chance at a new life. Thank you." His voice broke on the last word, and I reached over and hugged him again.

We became lost in our own thoughts. I reflected on what a bizarre, challenging thing family can be. Sometimes we keep secrets to protect the ones we love, to protect our family name, or to protect our family shame. Sometimes topics or incidents are verboten because they're too painful, the grief too powerful. The common denominator was all families have things they prefer to keep hidden.

As the lights dimmed, I leaned closer to him and whispered, "Maybe the reality is we can never truly escape our past or our family history. All we can do is decide how to move forward with the truth of it."

His eyes held mine briefly and then we directed our attention to the stage.

There was excited murmuring throughout as Ethan discussed the findings and how they'd been hidden all those years between the pages of the sheet music. Images of each letter were projected on the screen, and Ethan discussed the content of each and how much they added to what they knew of the Monroes' relationship. He pointed to the exchange of thoughts and ideas between Elizabeth and James, which no doubt influenced his perspective and policies. He added that the content of the letters also contributed to the general knowledge of how people lived during the Early Republic era and the impact the events of the day had on people's lives.

The presentation ended with Ethan offering gratitude to all who had been part of the process of the discovery.

"We'd like to offer a posthumous thank you to Mrs. Agnes Holt and Miss Mabel Murray for having taken such good care of the book over the years. Additionally, the museum offers a debt of gratitude to Mark Murray, who discovered a letter from his ancestor Mrs. Margaret Moray, who befriended Elizabeth Monroe here in Fredericksburg in 1786. Margaret's letter led to this historic discovery."

He scanned the room for Mark and finally found him next to me. Ethan smiled at him, then me.

"And to Ms. Olivia Wilde, budding private detective, whose valuable insights and keen observational skills helped lead to the discovery of the letters when Mr. Murray and I had thought we were at a dead end."

There was a quiet groan from somewhere behind me, but I didn't look around as Ethan continued.

"Finally, an enormous debt of gratitude to the Fredericksburg Police Department and especially the incomparable Detective Gina Gomez who helped bring the hunt for the letters to a safe conclusion."

A huge round of applause went up for all those he'd thanked.

A reception in the lobby followed the presentation, where Mark was swarmed by reporters. He seemed flustered and occasionally offended by their questions, but mostly happy.

Claire wandered over to say hello. "At least there was a happy ending," she said while hugging me.

"Yes, it does my heart good to see him smile."

We watched Mark field questions from reporters. After a while, I asked Claire something that had been bothering me since they discovered the letters.

"Why didn't Mark just wait until the books were at the museum? Couldn't he have examined them all he wanted to once they were there?"

"I've wondered the same thing." She glanced furtively around. When she spoke again, it was more quietly. "And there's been a fair amount of speculation about it among the staff. There are two main theories going around. One is he couldn't risk Ethan seeing the books first and finding the letters before he could. The second theory is if someone officially donated the books to the museum, there would've been acquisition forms to be filled out, which would include a pretty detailed description of the books. So, if he made any alterations to them, like pulling off the paper on the inside of the cover or removing the bookplates, someone would notice. Plus, there are security cameras in several places in the museum, including in the archives in the basement. So, if there'd been any suspicion directed at him, all they would've needed to do was review the recordings from those cameras and they would've seen him tampering with the books."

It felt so contradictory to see him now, smiling and calm, and remember him on the bridge or envision him plotting to steal the books.

Claire must have been having similar thoughts. "I still find it hard to believe."

A fellow museum guide called her name from across the lobby and she said goodbye and wandered off.

I remained where I was, watching the crowd and wondering how many of them were there because they were genuinely excited about the letters and how many of them were there for the juicy gossip continuing to fly around town.

There was a tap on my shoulder. Sophie and Jane stood beside me, each with a glass of wine in their hands.

"I didn't know you guys were here. How'd I miss you?" I hugged them, happy to find someone to stand with on the outskirts of the crowd.

"I snuck in after it began. I wasn't sure I wanted to show my face," said Sophie.

She'd been reprimanded at the library but had argued her actions were not strictly against library policy, since there was no specific policy about it—though I'd bet there was one now. Whether it was the lack of policy or the skeletons in the closet she knew of, or more likely, that it all got resolved to the library's benefit, nothing much had changed for her at work.

"And I was inclined to avoid the whole circus. I've had enough excitement for one year," Jane said.

"Have you?" Sophie asked. There was something in her tone that caught my attention.

I was going to follow up on it when someone cleared their throat behind us. We turned to find a handsome young man with shaggy brown hair and green eyes. He nodded at Jane and offered his arm. She accepted it and strode off with him toward the tables of food, with a quick, apologetic but happy smile over her shoulder at me.

I looked at Sophie with surprise. She took my arm just as Jane had done, and whispered, "His name is Spencer."

I grinned as I watched them walk away.

Sophie and I surveyed crowd together for a while, but I soon found her watching me with a mischievous smile.

"So, a budding private detective, huh?"

"Whatever," I said dismissively.

"Don't scoff. It's a brilliant idea," she said. She sipped her wine and then said, "You can call it G.G. Investigations."

A voice cut through the sound of Sophie's laughter. "Don't encourage her."

Gomez approached, wearing a stylish black pantsuit. She was pretty when she wasn't being so stern.

"Ah, so it was you groaning in the back of the room when Ethan called me a detective. Now, I understand," I said.

She smiled genuinely at me.

"Gina Gomez, huh?"

I was hit with a sense of premonition when Sophie and I simultaneously said, "G.G.," much to Gomez's mortification.

CHAPTER TWENTY-SIX

B y the time our Monthly in September rolled around, things had finally started to settle down around the story of the letters. I was anticipating a fun, relaxed evening with the ladies. It was Sophie's month to host—her husband, Ben, and their two sons were banished to the basement for the night. They lived in an early 1900s, pale yellow, wood frame house on Charlotte Street with a beautiful front porch that also wrapped around the left side.

They'd refinished the basement, so it wasn't like the creepy basement in my old house, which had been alive with those terrifying camel crickets. Having a nice basement meant it wasn't a punishment for her family to have to hang out there for the evening. Whenever it was Sophie's turn to host our gathering, they made it into a special night of their own with pizza and a movie.

When I arrived, Claire and Mary were sitting on the porch swing, enjoying the warm evening and glasses of wine. I'd made potato salad to go along with our main course of barbecued ribs. I dropped it off in the kitchen before joining the ladies on the porch. The scent of the ribs cooking made my mouth water. Sophie was known for her homemade, sweet, honey barbecue sauce.

I poured myself a glass of Chardonnay from the selection of beverages arrayed on a table and sat in a rocking chair. Claire and Mary smiled and after we'd exchanged greetings I asked Claire, "Any word from Mark? Is he making progress on his book?"

"He's been by the museum several times to reread the letters. He has the scans of them, but the history nerd in him can't resist seeing them in person."

"He must be horrified they were almost lost for good that night on the bridge," I said.

"Oh, my. I hadn't even thought of all the history that could have been lost," Mary said.

Claire added quietly, "We could have lost much more."

Her gaze was so intent I was at a loss for words. Finally, she broke eye contact, her brow furrowed.

"What are you thinking, Claire? Or don't I want to know?" I asked.

She hesitated; her expression so serious it prompted Mary to put her hand on top of Claire's.

"What is it?" Mary asked.

Claire's voice was thick with emotion when she spoke again. "I haven't been able to stop wondering how the night might've played out differently if it had been Jonathan out there on the bridge, or any black man being pursued by the police."

Neither Mary nor I responded right away. I hated to admit it was a thought that hadn't occurred to me, but I admitted it anyway.

"I hadn't thought about that." I felt angry at myself when I realized Claire didn't have the luxury of not thinking about it.

The silence lingered until I said, "I believe Detective Gomez would've been fair and compassionate no matter who was on the bridge. But it's a question I'm glad we didn't have to find out the answer to."

They simply let the swing float forward and backward.

Claire made no apology for sharing something difficult. She knew she didn't need to.

The three of us sat silently together, lost in our own thoughts. My thoughts left me wondering how much fear Claire lives with on a daily basis that she never shares with us.

As if hearing my thoughts, Mary put her arm around Claire's shoulders and Claire let her head fall against Mary. They sat there leaning on each other, letting the fear and the friendship hold them, just as they held each other.

I was hesitant to interrupt the silence, but I had a question, and as our expert on all things relating to the people of Fredericksburg, Mary was the person to ask. "Mary?"

She lifted her head but kept her arm around Claire.

"Did you know anything about Mark's family before all this?"

She hesitated, which was unusual for Mary. Claire raised herself off Mary's shoulder so she could see her.

"Yes, I'd heard rumors." Mary said quietly.

We waited for her to continue, but she was reluctant.

Finally, she went on. "I never knew many details about his family, only that the name Murray was not exactly held in high regard."

"Not exactly held in high regard?"

She sighed. "It's a small community in a lot of ways, which as you know has its benefits and its downsides. Some of those downsides were greater in the past, unfortunately. We're human and are susceptible to groupthink." She shrugged apologetically. "It's not an excuse, just an explanation. I don't know what else to say."

She focused on the porch floor drifting by under her feet and continued, "I asked Momma about them after what happened on the bridge. She told me Mark's mom lost their home not long after his father died. She wasn't able to get help from any of the local banks, and they weren't regular churchgoers. I wish . . ." Her voice trailed off.

It was quiet except for the sound of the squeak of the chains on the hooks supporting the porch swing until Claire perked up.

"Why only wish?"

She had our attention.

"Why not change the groupthink?" Claire asked. "There has to be something we can do. It can't be too late to help Mark and his mom and try to make up for the past at least a little. He must've had to hire a lawyer and has legal fees to pay. We could start there."

Mary perked up and kissed Claire on the cheek. "You have a kind and brilliant heart. We can definitely find a way to help."

Mary quickly sent out a flurry of texts to rally her Fredericksburg connections to help Mark and his mom. It made my heart happy to see.

Claire and I sipped our wine while Mary was typing away on her phone. We greeted Hannah when she arrived with a tray full of mac and cheese. Everyone had arrived except Jane.

"Has anyone heard from Jane?" I asked.

Sophie stepped out onto the porch with a sly grin and casually said, "I asked her to pick something up for me on her way over." When she directed her smile at me, I didn't need to be a psychic to predict I wasn't going to like whatever it was.

"It's not a new python to add the family, is it?" asked Mary with a shudder.

"Or a friend of Spencer's for each of us?" Hannah asked hopefully, standing in the doorway behind Sophie.

"Ha. I would love another python," said Sophie enthusiastically. "But Ben's not likely to get on board with the idea." He was not a big fan of Sophie's beloved ball python, Kaa. "Or the friend of Spencer's suggestion either, unfortunately." She smirked.

It occurred to me fleetingly that a snake would've been a good way to keep the camel cricket population down in my old basement, but I didn't let it distract me from Sophie's statement about Jane. "So, what's she really picking up?"

"You'll have to wait and see," she said mysteriously.

I didn't have to wait long. Jane soon arrived and squeezed into the last parking spot across the street. Sophie's neighbors must hate it when she hosts our gatherings and we take up all the best parking spots on the block.

Sophie ran down the steps of the porch and across the street to meet Jane. When they walked into the yard, Sophie was carrying a large, rectangular box with a cellophane panel in the top and Jane was carrying a nondescript brown paper bag with a handle.

Sophie was grinning from ear to ear like the proverbial cat who'd swallowed the canary, while Jane was wearing the cat. She had on her new t-shirt featuring Cosmo the Cougar, mascot of Brigham Young University. After everyone had found out about her and Spencer, we gave it to her as a gift from all of us at the last Monthly. It made it even more fun knowing BYU's founder would not approve of Jane's behavior.

When we'd grilled her for details on Spencer at previous Monthlies, Jane said he'd been so mortified by his previous behavior he'd avoided her when he came home. She said he was more mature now.

I didn't know if it was true or how long it might last, but she'd certainly been happier for the past few months.

Mary had jumped up as they approached and was holding the front door open for Sophie and Jane, who went inside without stopping. I glanced at Hannah and Claire hoping for an explanation, but they smiled and shrugged, feigning ignorance.

I went into the house, not knowing what to expect. When I reached the dining room, I found Sophie and Jane standing on the far side of the table with the box and the bag sitting in front of them. While Sophie poured them glasses of wine, everyone else gathered around.

Sophie tapped her wine glass with a fork as if preparing for a speech. "Tonight, we raise our glasses to endings and beginnings." She held up a glass of wine in front of her and we all did the same.

She addressed Jane. "First, to the end of our trust in our beloved Jane, because she can clearly keep secrets from us far better than we ever thought possible."

We all laughed, including Jane.

"But also, to the new beginning for her and Spencer."

Claire chimed in, "Three roars for Jane!"

We all drank a toast to Jane, who was embarrassed and a little pleased.

Next, Sophie raised her glass to Claire. "To both endings and new beginnings for the staff of the James Monroe Museum."

We raised our glasses more solemnly, but Claire added, "And to the beginning of newfound and well-deserved fame for James and Elizabeth Monroe."

That made us all smile.

Then Sophie turned to me. I felt a touch of anxiety and heat rising in my cheeks, which for once had nothing to do with a hot flash. "Finally, to Liv and G.G.! The game's afoot!"

"The game's afoot," they all shouted while raising their glasses.

With their glasses still in the air, Jane reached into the bag and produced a pipe and Sherlock Holmes-inspired deerstalker hat, and Sophie opened the box to reveal a sheet cake with the same hat and pipe drawn with icing and the words, *G.G. Investigations* written in bright red.

For a second, I saw a flash of Gomez's face in my mind, but it disappeared as Jane came around the table and placed the hat on my head and pipe in my hand. I laughed until I cried.

At the end of evening, we were back on the porch with our wine glasses in hand. I had snagged a seat on the swing with Sophie, and we held hands as we let the swing drift gently to-and-fro.

Taking in the scene, I was overcome with gratitude for the safe space we'd created together for laughter and friendship, disagreements and difficult questions, and for supporting each other's dreams, whether or not we thought they were ludicrous.

AUTHOR'S NOTE

I wrote *Flashes of Insight* in part because I found that no one, not even my girlfriends who have helped me through every challenge in my life, wanted to talk with me about perimenopause when the symptoms began. I tried to start a discussion/commiseration group. Two people showed up for the first gathering and we never had another meeting. It was a topic people were clearly reluctant to talk about and yet, one which could have such a significant impact on our lives.

It is my hope, therefore, that this book will spark conversations among women, between women and men, and heck, even among men, about the symptoms, difficulties, and benefits (there are one or two) of perimenopause and menopause. I hope it will initiate discussions that can be both honest and humorous. We can learn from each other's experiences and walk through the natural changes more gracefully together.

One of the best things I did for myself during perimenopause, was to christen my moody personality Grumpy Gal or G.G. It offered me a way to bring some levity to the situation, but also to reclaim the internal power I felt was draining away through the hormonal shifts. I felt as if not only my moods, but so many things about my body were out of my control. Giving the moodiness a name that made me smile helped me refocus on the moment and was a reminder I could still choose how I wanted to react to what was happening, whether it was a hot flash or a grumpy mood. I could breathe through the sweatiness, acknowledge what was happening, and make a choice about how I wanted to proceed at that moment. To be honest, some days that meant just allowing myself to cry or rant about what was happening, rather than peacefully accept it. It was important for me to remember any of those reactions were OK, as long as no one was harmed in the course of my ranting! The most important thing, though, was to recognize that I had a choice. It made all the difference for me.

I hope this book will remind women moving through any hormonal changes in their lives, that while some days are difficult, you can do hard things with humor, grace, and a little G.G. attitude. If there are days you don't think you can muster the strength for doing hard things, remember, sometimes grace and strength look exactly like reaching out for help from a friend, a family member, or a counselor.

~ell~

While, like Liv, I'm originally from south Jersey, I've lived in Fredericksburg for 28 years. It is my home. It has been a wonderful place to raise my daughters, do a lot of growing myself, make lifelong friends, explore the Rappahannock River, and so much more. It's one of my favorite places on earth, and while in Liv's fictional version of Fredericksburg, the small-town atmosphere proves to be a challenge for the antagonist, I have found it to be a supportive and loving community. If you haven't visited our small city before, I hope you'll put it on your list of places to visit. Here you will find an abundance of historic sites, good food, amazing art, beautiful river vistas, and fabulous people!

Acknowledgements

Bringing a book to life requires not just a writer with an imagination, but a whole community of people supporting that writer. It would be impossible to truly express the depth of my gratitude to everyone who helped me on this journey in big and small ways, but I will at least make a beginning.

First and foremost, my deepest thanks are to my beloved husband Bill, who is the one who had to move through perimenopause with me and G.G. on a daily basis. Luckily for me, he learned to embrace her just as I did. I will be applying for sainthood for him soon.

Any book is written for readers, and I had some wonderful people who read the manuscript in its various stages and offered helpful feedback. The very first person I dared share it with was Heidi Stello, who not only offered feedback on the story, but who was also my consultant on all things Monroe. Other early readers were Kathy Ryback, Kymn Harvin, Sharon Babineau, Vicki Killen, Martina McGowan, Pat Coate, Lillian Allen, James Allen, Carol Nicholson, Jessica Utz, Lucy Utz, Bill Brooks, Lee Criscuolo, Suzy Stone, and Debby Scott.

This book would not exist without the treasured female friends throughout my life who taught me that life is infinitely richer with women I can talk with, laugh with, swear with, be myself with, get into a little trouble with, grow with, and grieve with. Thank you, Christine, Carol, Ann, Debra, Mauri, Sharon, Lori, Morgan, Charlotte, Anne, LaDell, Kathleen, Teresa, Nancy, Traci, Brenda, Julie, Marie, Jennifer, Susan, Xan, Sam, and all my Second Friday girlfriends. I'm also lucky enough to count my sisters Pat, Kathy, and Vicki, and my daughters as friends. Without all these women, the friendships portrayed in this, and future books, would not be as rich and without my daughters, there would have been no drama flag!

I participated in a variety of creative groups throughout the process of writing this book. The participants in those groups offered moral support, feedback, cheerleading, inspiration, and friendship, all of which were invaluable. The leader of those groups was the talented and kindhearted Mary Anne em Radmacher. Her friendship and inspiration helped me make the leap that made this book possible. My deep thanks to the other members of the groups including Jean Martell, Jeanette Richardson Herring, Marci Moore, Pam Williams, Heather Mack, Ann Bell, Susan Paul Johnson, Kymn Harvin, Candace Doby, Karen Anderson, Ann Ellinger Magee, Muse Sawyer, Martina McGowan, and Liz Amaya-Fernandez.

Being a member of a mystery writers' group helped me in a variety of ways, including feedback, commiseration, inspiration, guidance, and friendship. Thank you to the Royals for all the above. A special thanks to Lane Stone for welcoming me into the fold and to Ellen Butler for advice and guidance on being an independent author.

Fellow writer and friend, J.S. Furlong, provided valuable insights into being an indie author, encouragement, and excellent feedback on the story.

Assistance with research for various elements of the story was provided by the kind staff at the Historic Fredericksburg Foundation, Inc., Sue Bridi, Joy O'Toole at the Central Rappahannock Regional Library, David R. Hines, Sheriff Hanover County Virginia, Brian Layton, Fredericksburg Chief of Police, Betsy Mason, Fredericksburg Deputy Chief of Police, and Heidi Stello, Associate Editor of The Papers of James Monroe.

I'm grateful to my friends and former colleagues at the James Monroe Museum. My time working for the museum provided part of the inspiration for this story. All JMM employees (current and former) hope a secret cache of letters between James and Elizabeth Monroe will be found one day. So, check your attics!

Thanks are also due to the many professionals who have helped move the book from dream to reality. I worked with a variety of editors and proofreaders at various stages of the manuscript who helped me both craft a better story and improve my grammar, which was no small feat! My thanks to Clair Lamb, Paula J. Kelly, J.D. Hildebrand, Barbara Grassey, Joan Gelfand, Austin Camacho, and Tom Allen. Thank you to Ryan Fox for his help with legal matters. I'm grateful to Laura Boyle for the wonderful cover and for her grace. It's not just anyone who can distill the essence of a story into a single image. Marketing assistance from Kristen O'Connell, Maria Carola, and Nancy Findley has been essential in helping me get the book ready for launch and into your hands. Sarah Mattingly's skills as a photographer made me feel comfortable in front of a camera, which was miraculous!

It was my mom who instilled a love of books in me from a young age. Thank you, Mom. Because of her, before I even dreamed of being an author, I was an enthusiastic reader. The first mysteries I remember reading were written by Phyllis Whitney, who I had the pleasure of meeting. It was a joy to have the opportunity to tell her how much I loved her books as a teenager.

As a reader myself, my final thanks must go to you, dear reader, for picking up (or downloading) this book and for your own love of reading.

Other Titles by Lynda Allen

Check www.lyndaallenwrites.com for announcements about
the second Liv Wilde mystery at the end of 2024!

Poetry
Grace Reflected
Wild Divinity
Illumine
Rest in the Knowing

Nonfiction
The Rules of Creation

ABOUT THE AUTHOR

Photo credit: Sarah Mattingly

Lynda Allen began her career in video post-production and documentary filmmaking before focusing her knack for storytelling on writing. She is the author of four poetry collections, *Rest in the Knowing*, *Illumine*, *Wild Divinity*, and *Grace Reflected*. She has also published *The Rules of Creation (nonfiction)*. *Flashes of Insight* is the first book in her Liv Wilde mystery series.

Lynda proudly infuses her fiction writing with her Jersey girl sensibilities and aims to create stories imbued with heart and humor. She lives near the banks of the Rappahannock River in Fredericksburg, VA with her husband, their cats, and the many incredible eagle friends who pay them frequent visits.

Sign up for Lynda's newsletter at

www.lyndaallenwrites.com

or use the QR code below.

Made in the USA
Columbia, SC
06 April 2024

34072338R00176